BOOK TWO

Reaper

A DARK MAFIA ROMANCE

CHELLE ROSE

CW01497100

Bonetti Brothers Series Book Two © 2024 Chelle Rose
All rights reserved under the International and Pan-American
Copyright Conventions. No part of this book may be reproduced or
transmitted in any form or by any means, electronic or mechanical,
including photocopying, recording, or by any information storage
and retrieval system, without permission in writing from the
publisher.

Warning: the unauthorized reproduction or distribution of this
copyrighted work is illegal. Criminal copyright infringement,
including infringement without monetary gain, is investigated by the
FBI and is punishable by up to 5 years in prison and a fine of
$250,000. Printed in the United States of America.

This book is a work of fiction. Names, characters, places, and
incidents are the product of the author's imagination or are used
fictitiously. Any resemblance to actual events, locations, or persons,
living or dead, is coincidental. This book is intended for a mature
audience of 18+.

Cover Design and Interior Formatting RedFox Book Design
Editing by Furious Editing

All rights reserved. No part of this image may be reproduced,
scanned, transmitted, or distributed in any printed or electronic form
without permission.

Note to the Reader

Your mental health is important. Please don't read blind if you have any triggers! You can find them here:

DEDICATION:

To those of you who embrace things others run from.
Good girl. Let the darkness in. Don't fight it. I promise it'll feel
good.

Chapter One

REAPER

They never get away from me, only her. One might think she's smarter than the rest since she escaped, but in the end, it won't make a difference. Her one mistake was leaving her purse behind when she ran for her life, because now I know who she is and where she lives.

Arabella Riley.

Birthdate: May 21, 2005.

Address: 1624 Ninth Street. Apartment B4.

She made this so easy, and it makes me want to punish her. What if some other man had found this? Did she not consider how much danger she could be in?

I chuckle to myself because, of course, she's in a world of trouble once I get my hands on her.

They say the eyes are the window to the soul. It's the reason I do the things I do. Every set of eyes are beautiful as life evaporates from them. I've never wanted to keep eyes after ending a life. Arabella will be the first. I've already researched how to preserve them.

To preserve eyeballs, or any other organ or specimen, in a wet jar method, inject it with formalin. Then place the injected specimen in a jar of the same solution of formalin for a few days, or weeks. Even months, depending on the size of your specimens.

The problem for me is, months, or weeks, will not suffice. I want to keep them forever. I never want those pretty blue eyes to fade away. Sometimes plans need to change. If she cooperates, maybe I'll let her live, so I can always have her gaze on me.

I sit in the club where she dances with her friends. Arabella moves as if she doesn't have a care in the world. Hands in her long blonde hair, swaying those hips like she's doing it just for me. Is she trying to taunt me? Add that to the list of reasons to hurt her.

Sweet, living dead girl. Tonight you will come face to face with the man that has become your greatest fear. You'll make a choice. Be mine or die. Either I'll get to see her eyes on me while I fuck her, or I'll look into them and squeeze the life out of her delicate body.

She stands with two girls on either side of her, two brunettes, but I barely notice them. My attention is completely focused on my living dead girl. Arabella tosses back her third drink of the night. Big mistake. She is going to need all her wits to get through the night, and the alcohol isn't going to help her. A man approaches her with a drink, and I'm done watching. I'm a Bonetti, and though I don't currently work with the family, my name still carries weight. I can do nearly anything I want in this club with little interference, including dragging Arabella out by her gorgeous blonde head of hair. And the fucker coming on to my girl? His night is going to be short, along with his life. What did he do to deserve to die? Touching what's mine is his crime. For that, he'll pay with his life. I've killed for far less. Most of the time, there is nothing they've done to deserve it.

I wade through the crowd of drunk gyrating assholes, spilling more than one drink, as I approach the douchebag, but not giving a fuck. Her back is turned to me, so she has no idea I'm here. Stopping behind the blonde guy with his hand on her shoulder, I growl, "Get your hands off my property."

Arabella turns to the sound of my voice with a start, and instantly turns so pale she looks like a fucking ghost. A beautiful ghost. The fear in her eyes probably shouldn't make my dick anywhere near as hard as it does. Her ocean blue gaze widens, as I swear she has a cartoon bubble over her head saying, 'Run!'

I chuckle as I narrow my gaze at her. "Did you think I forgot about you, baby?"

The stupid man standing next to her glares at me and asks, "Do you want me to get rid of him?"

2

I laugh obnoxiously, because I'd really fucking like to see him try.

Reaching around him, I grab his throat and squeeze hard, knowing he's freaking out because he can't breathe. Every living creature reacts the same way from lack of oxygen. It's as if I can physically see the panic. He grabs at my hand, trying to pull it away. His eyes widen. The fear is visceral. And intoxicating.

Removing my hand from his throat, he coughs and gasps as he rubs the front of his throat, trying to ease the pain. He hacks again, as he gulps in the air he desperately needs.

"This is how this is going to go. You're both coming with me or I'll kill you right here, in front of God and everybody. The hundreds of witnesses won't deter me, because every cop in this fucking city is owned by my family."

My brother, Bones, is the head of the family, and killing two people with so many witnesses will definitely result in a lecture. However, he'd have my back, the same way I'd have his. They glance at each other, and Arabella nods at her friend and says, "He isn't kidding. Do what he says."

I shove him in the direction of the back door and follow, watching them both closely, living dead girl more than him, because fuck me, she's gorgeous. The only thing about her more stunning than her eyes is that ass that moves the exact right amount when she walks.

After opening the front door to my truck, I point for her to get inside, before handcuffing her wrist to the oh shit handle, because I already know she's likely to run if she gets the opportunity. I push blondie into the back seat and zip tie his hands behind his back, as well as around his ankles, and seatbelt him in, because safety is important.

I chuckle to myself after I close their doors, and make it to the driver's side and climb in. Arabella speaks as soon as I pull away. I love her voice, so soft and sweet, but she clearly thinks I'm an idiot.

3

I know the part where you're supposed to humanize yourself with your would-be killer.

"My name is Arabella. But everybody calls me Bella. I don't think we properly introduced ourselves before. I'm nineteen. I work in a coffee shop and I'm in college."

I turn out of the parking lot as she continues, "I'm young. I want to live. I'll do whatever you say."

Smirking at her, I say, "I knew all of that already, living dead girl."

She shifts uncomfortably in her seat with her arm stretched in the air. "What's your name?"

I glance in the mirror, watching to make sure blondie doesn't surprise me. It's hard with all four of your limbs restrained, but I've seen stranger things. His eyes are wide with terror as he stares out the window like there's a way out. There isn't. Tonight he dies.

"They call me Reaper."

Arabella raises her eyebrow and asks, "What's your real name?"

I make a left turn while I consider whether or not I should tell her. She isn't leaving alive so it doesn't matter, especially because what will she do? Go to the police?

"Nico. Nico Bonetti."

"Nico," she repeats, like she's trying my name out on her tongue. And I don't hate it. Somehow, I think any word coming out of her mouth would be sexy as hell. I make a mental note to make her beg. Fuck, I should put a metal collar around her slender neck, and walk her on a fucking leash. I've never done that before, but she makes me want to. This woman makes me crave things I never have, and that alone makes her dangerous. I should end her life and be done with it.

"Nico, please don't kill me."

I glance at her as I pull into the empty parking lot for the lake in the middle of nowhere. That's why we're here, because I knew no one would be here at this time.

After putting the truck in park, I open my door and whistle as I walk to her door and open it. Her blue eyes, filled with fear, stare at me and fuck, I've missed it. Rubbing my thumb over her bottom lip, I groan, because she drives me crazy.

"Are you going to cry for him when he dies?"

"No," she whispers.

I take in all her features as I ask her, "Will you beg for me to spare his life?"

She shakes her head lightly. "I will only beg for mine."

Stroking my fingers down her cheek, I tell her, "If you want to prolong your life, you'll keep your eyes on mine while I end his."

This will be the first time I've ever not looked into someone's eyes while killing them, but I can't help myself. Her eyes are far more appealing than his are.

I push her seat back, and grab her hips and rotate her, so she's able to see into the backseat. This is a test. A big fucking test. I'm about to see what my living dead girl is made of. If she screams and cries, then I know to kill her soon. If she shows me she's stronger than she appears, I might keep her a bit longer. Maybe forever.

Chapter Two

BELLA

There is no way I'm begging for him to spare his life. Jeff is an asshole anyway. Nobody will miss him, least of all me. That's not why I won't ask for Reaper to let him live though. I'm going to save all his kindness, if he has any, for myself.

I sit on my knees watching the backseat as he climbs in beside Jeff. I keep my eyes on him like he demanded, because I don't want to die. Reaper gets onto his knees beside Jeff and wraps his gloved hand around his throat, without taking his eyes from mine.

"Normally, I don't do this quickly, but there are things I'd rather be doing."

He stares at me with a heated expression while he squeezes the life out of Jeff. If he hadn't tried to kill me, he would be attractive. His chiseled jaw and dark eyes draw me in, but it's the way his throat moves when he swallows that makes me clench my thighs, even though I should be dry as a bone. The muscles in his arms bulge, and he has my full attention, causing me to ignore Jeff's strangled sounds.

"Eyes on me, Bella."

He tried to kill me once and he probably will again. Reaper is wearing black jeans and a black t-shirt, and I try to keep my eyes on his but, against my will, they move back to his arms, and I watch his muscles contract with the force of him crushing Jeff's windpipe. While it shouldn't be, the power in his hands is a turn on. My clit pulses as I watch Nico do the one thing no human being has a right to do.

Jeff struggles beneath Reaper, trying to get free, but he doesn't even come close. With his hands bound behind his back, he never stood a chance. With the strength Reaper clearly has, without breaking a sweat, I'm not sure, if he had the use of his hands, that he would've managed to save his life anyway. I get the feeling if Reaper decides you die, you do.

Reaper releases his grip on Jeff, and I glance at his open, unblinking eyes, before looking back to Reaper. He winks at me. "I'll be back."

After undoing the seat belt, he climbs out of the car and pulls Jeff's dead body out, lifts him over his shoulder, and walks off into a wooded area. I shift in my seat so I'm facing the front window and wait for him to come back, as I try to think of how I can make him choose to let me live. I don't know what this guy's story is, but I do know killing people is not a hardship for him. I sit handcuffed to his truck, and think back to the night we met, if you want to call it that.

A man I've never met stares at me with a clenched jaw, as he waits for his black coffee. Do I know him? I don't think so, but the way his eyes focus on me suggests otherwise. I hand him his drink, but he doesn't say a word. Silently, he puts a fifty-dollar bill in my tip jar, and turns and walks away. After finishing my shift, I grab my purse and head home. I wave goodbye to Jessie and walk out the door. I don't live far from work, so I don't worry too much about my safety but, having to walk down a dark alleyway littered with drug paraphernalia, and the occasional dealer hanging around, does make me slightly nervous. I do the same thing I do every night. I pay attention to my surroundings and move quickly. There's nobody out here tonight. Not a single homeless person, just me. The silence is eerie, like in a horror movie, before the killer gets to the pretty blonde girl, who isn't paying attention to what's going on around her. A shiver crawls down my skin as a hand reaches into my hair, and pulls me backward. He places a hand over my mouth, stifling my scream, and growls into my ear.

"All people are beautiful when they die, but you, you're going to be my favorite."

8

Grabbing my shoulders, he spins me around so I'm facing him, and I tremble as I beg him for my life.

"Take whatever you want, but please don't kill me."

I tilt my head up and look into his eyes with a gasp, as realization dawns on me. It's my customer from the coffee shop. Did he follow me?

He tracks his thumb through my fallen tears, and groans like he enjoys making me cry.

"There is only one thing I want from you. Your life."

"Please. I didn't do anything to deserve this."

He chuckles. "They rarely do."

Winding my hair around his fist, he pulls me to a truck blocking the alleyway.

"We can do this the easy way or the hard way. Either way, we're doing it."

Opening the passenger door to the truck, he waves me in. My mom once told me about this episode she once saw on Oprah. Never go to a second location. I don't see many options though. There's nowhere for me to run to here. If I refuse, he'll probably kill me right here.

"Having to repeat myself makes me angry. I suggest you do as you're told, or this will become unpleasant."

"Become?" I snort as I climb into the truck, because this has not exactly been a pleasant experience thus far.

He gets into the truck, and starts driving, with an unreadable expression on his face. Whoever this man is, he's quiet, rarely speaking to me, but frequently staring at me. He only takes his eyes off me to look at where he's going. It's creepy at best.

My killer pulls off the main road over loose gravel, and I look up so I can see where we are. A fucking graveyard? You've got to be kidding me. I'm not one of these people creeped out by a cemetery under normal circumstances. However, considering he's planning to kill me, I'm fucking terrified. This guy is nuts. And I know if I don't do something to save myself, he's going to end my life

Chapter Three
REAPER (PAST)

Instead of being completely terrified, she appeared slightly scared. It piqued my curiosity about this woman. Pulling into my family cemetery changed everything for her, which wasn't really the goal, but I suppose it works, because I do want her fear. Killing people isn't about terrifying people, not for me, anyway. It's about the power in my hands, and watching life leave their eyes. Yet when she realized I was going to kill her, the way her eyes widened with terror was truly beautiful. I've never seen eyes like hers before. Of course, I've watched more than one set of blue eyes fade as they died. Hers are different, and it's what drew me to her. It's what made the compulsion I have come out to play. My pretty dead girl has light blue eyes on the outside, but the closer they get to her pupil, the darker they get. They are fucking fascinating, and since the moment my gaze met hers, I've wondered what they'd look like when she takes her final breath. Tonight, I'll find out.

I park and open my door, and order her, "Stay."

She rolls her eyes, and I smirk to myself. I think she's going to be a fighter. Fuck, I haven't had a fighter in so long. Someone that will scratch and claw me, trying to save their life. Everybody is afraid of death, but they don't realize I'm probably giving them a gift. They should be thanking me, because this world fucking sucks.

Walking around to her side, I open the door. "Are you religious?"

"What?"

I chuckle at her confused expression.

"Are you religious? We can do this by one of the crosses."

She looks so pretty as she chews on her bottom lip, nervous, but trying to look brave, and then she rolls her stunning eyes at me. Fucking perfect.

"I wish I were. Right now, I wish I believed in something. If only there was an all powerful God that would strike you down."

I stroke my fingers down her face, enjoying her softness under my calloused skin. She really is beautiful.

Taking her hand in mine, ignoring the warmth of our hands together, I take her over to my favorite headstone. It's my Aunt Eva's, and it's worn from so much time, but it's beautiful. Grayed stone with a cross at the top, and across the middle it says, 'you'll live forever in our hearts', written in Italian. Aunt Eva was my dad's sister, and she passed away as a young child so I never met her.

"Lay down. Over the grave."

She does as she's told, pulling her black skirt down to not expose herself to me. She looks stunning, lying in wait for her life to end. She wears a white button-down shirt that's her work uniform. This isn't about sex for me. I never even have the urge, but I do right now. I want to feel her from the inside, to stretch her wide, but I won't.

I climb over her, and stare at her tear-streaked cheeks, before looking into her eyes. Wrapping my hand around her throat, I squeeze as she struggles. She turns her head, and bites my wrist until she draws blood. She was probably hoping I'd remove my hand, and let her run away, but I don't. I tighten my grip, as I watch the panic in her gaze grow by the second. And just like that, she's gone, and I'm instantly filled with regret. It didn't feel like it's supposed to, and much to my brother's annoyance, I still haven't figured out what I want to do with her body. Again, I'll need to call him for help. Of course, he'll help me, but he'll be pissed at me.

Chapter Four

REAPER (PAST)

She lays on the ground, eyes wide open, beautiful blue eyes. I haven't checked her pulse, but I know she's dead. I can't stop staring at her pale skin as my brother approaches me.

"What the fuck," Bones says, like he didn't know I'd be here with a dead body.

With my eyes focused on the most beautiful creature I've ever seen, I ask him the question that burns through me.

"Isn't she pretty? I think I want to keep her eyes. That's not weird, right?"

"Jesus Christ. You're the one we should call Psycho. Yeah, it's a little fucking weird, man."

His response lets me know he definitely thinks it's weird, but I can't let her go. I've never done anything like keeping eyes before. I know most serial killers keep souvenirs, I do not. I've never wanted to. And now it's too late.

"Look, if you're going to kill people, you need to learn to dispose of the bodies. You can't be calling me at all hours of the damn night for help."

I nod slowly. "I know."

Bones leans up against a gravestone. "Alright, you need to figure out a way to ditch the bodies, but make sure they won't be found until the DNA has degraded enough that there's no evidence. Or better yet, destroy the evidence."

I scratch my dark hair. "What if I buy a farm?"

"Reaper, can we focus? I don't care if you buy a farm, but you need to deal with your dead girl first."

Not taking my eyes from her, I sneer, "I've done some research. A pig can eat a two hundred pound human in eight minutes."

My brother shakes his head at me with disgust. "Is that so, Reaper? Well, you've got it all figured out then, don't you? Do you know they can't digest teeth? Hair? They leave them behind. Do you know what they use teeth and hair for, Reaper?"

My brother nods, with a smug expression on his face that does little, other than annoy me. "That's right, brother. DNA. Evidence. If anybody ever looks on your hypothetical farm, they'll find DNA evidence proving that you knew the dead girl."

The not so dead girl blinks rapidly, and jumps to her feet with a terrified scream.

Fuck!

She runs like her life depends on it, and I suppose it does. Quickly, my victim bolts and disappears into the trees, while I chase after her. Whoever this woman is, she's good, because I can't find her anywhere, and the leaves that must be beneath her feet are silent. I listen in every direction, listening for the crunching, or a rock being kicked, since there's so much gravel here. But there's nothing. It's as if she flew away and I don't understand it. They never escape. I walk back over to where my brother is, and admit defeat, as I grab her purse from the ground. I'll find her, that's not even a question. Getting away from me prolonged her life, but it didn't save it. The only thing she accomplished, other than that, was creating an obsession deep inside me. They never get free from me and neither will she. I'll give her some time. When she begins to relax, and thinks I've forgotten about her, then I'll swoop in and finish what I started here tonight.

Chapter Five
BELLA (PRESENT)

Reaper comes back to the truck and gets in, turns the ignition, and takes off without a word. After nearly fifteen minutes of his silence, I can't take it any longer.

"Why do you want to kill me?"

He turns to me with a smirk. "Your eyes. I'm fascinated, and want to see what they'll look like when you die. I've never seen any more beautiful than yours."

I laugh, because what else can I do?

"If I die, my eyes will too."

If I have my way, I'll never see him again, but he can figure that out later.

"No. I'll keep them. Preserve them."

What? Did he just say he's going to kill me, but cut my eyeballs out and keep them? Like in a fucking jar or something? This guy is insane.

"Have you been diagnosed with a mental illness?"

It's probably a stupid question, because clearly there's something very wrong with him. Mentally balanced people do not want to kill someone and cut their eyes out. That's an extra special level of deranged.

He chuckles loudly. "You would think so, but nope. I'm as sane as the next guy."

I think that's debatable but I don't say so, mainly because it's unwise to agitate the man that wants to kill me. If I can delay it, maybe I can run again, but this time I will go far away. Somewhere he'll never find me.

"You didn't scream," he says as he turns onto the highway, "or cry," he adds.

I'm struggling with how much truth I should give this man that deserves none, but ultimately I think the more I get him talking, the better the chances of my survival.

"You'll probably do the same, but he tried to rape me."

He arches an eyebrow. "You think I'm going to fuck you, living dead girl?"

I shrug with my free arm, because I really don't know what his plans are, other than killing me.

Reaper chuckles softly. "You've never been safer than you are with me," then he adds, "Sexually speaking."

I turn my head to him in a quick movement, as I stare at him in shock.

"Oh my God. You're gay!"

He smirks at me. "No, I'm not gay. I've just never been with a woman."

"Have you been with a man?"

This time, he gives me a glare that makes a shiver travel down my spine.

"No. I told you, I'm not gay. I'm a goddamn virgin."

My killer is a virgin? I'm not sure why, because I don't know much about him, but this information shocks me to my core. If I could set aside the fact that he intends to kill me, he'd be hot. Bend me over and fuck me into oblivion hot.

"Why? You can't be super religious."

He chuckles. "I'm not. I've spent my entire life fascinated with ending lives. I'm not normal, if you haven't figured that out yet. It's not that I don't want to, but every time I'm with a woman, I end up killing her, so it has never happened."

I wince from the pain in my arm, from it being stuck in the air, handcuffed to the top of the car.

"This isn't necessary. I'm not running. You'll only find me again."

"We'll be where we are going soon, and then I'll undo the cuffs."

16

He takes the third exit off the highway. I'm trying to keep him talking to me, but also trying to be aware of landmarks so if I can run, I'll have an idea of what direction to go in. When I told him I wouldn't try to get away, I lied. I'm not going to sit around waiting for this psychopath to kill me.

"How many people have you killed?"

He shrugs like I asked his favorite color, and it means nothing.

"I haven't kept count, really. A hundred or so since I was nine years old."

"Nine!" I blurt out, clearly revealing my shock. How the hell does someone make their first kill at such a young age?

He nods, like he's proud of doing something so terrible as a child, when he should've been innocent.

"My family is a mafia family. Someone tried to hurt my mom. I wasn't going to allow that to happen. The first time I saw the light leave someone's eyes, it was powerful. Magical. I knew I'd do it again."

Again, I'm sure shock registers on my face.

"You're in the mafia?"

He chuckles as he pulls through a gate to a massive property.

"Not exactly. Apparently, I'm too unhinged for the mafia."

I can't help but laugh, because how can that be possible? Aren't they the worst of the worst? Involved in drugs, trafficking, and yes, murder. It seems to me he'd fit right in.

"Is this your house?"

He shakes his head.

"You ask a lot of questions, living dead girl."

After parking his truck, he gets out and comes around to my side, and undoes the handcuff holding my wrist up. I rub my sore skin, and he grabs my arm and yanks me out of the vehicle.

"You're hurting me, dick."

Narrowing his gaze at me, he smirks.

17

"You don't need to savor it. I promise you, there will be more where that came from."

"Great."

He chuckles like he is having a great time. I'm glad one of us is. He walks me through a long covered courtyard, and then into the huge gray stone covered house.

I try to get a look at the kitchen, as we walk through it, and then the living room, but he pulls me to a spiral staircase.

"Your house is nice. All two seconds you allowed me to see of it, anyway. Maybe next time."

Gripping my bicep tighter, he growls, "You won't be seeing it. Where you are going, you will die."

"No need to sugar-coat things, Nico. Just go ahead, and tell me how terrible things are going to get."

He yanks on my arm, and I trip on the steps, and he yells at me.

"Jesus. Can you fucking walk?"

Pulling me back to my feet, he stares into my eyes like he's inspecting them.

"Be more careful, please. I don't want your eyes to get scratched."

Right. Because he's going to fucking keep them. I'm trying hard to not be afraid, but I'd have to be as much of a psychopath as he is, for me to not be terrified right now.

"Please tell me you'll cut them out after I'm dead."

We make it to the top step, and he pulls me into a bedroom and throws me down on the bed, before moving me closer to the headboard. Pulling his handcuffs out of his pocket, he silently cuffs each of my hands, while he is over me, a leg on each side of my chest.

Do I notice how hard he is? Sick fucker.

He backs away from me and smiles a devious grin.

"That'll do until I get back with supplies. To answer your question, I think you have to be alive so they are living organs still. If I kill you first, I think they will look dull and gray."

18

So he's going to cut my eyeballs out of their sockets before he kills me. That sounds rather painless. Fucking fantastic.

Reaper winks at me, and if my hands were free, I would punch him in his ugly face.

Except it's not ugly, but I'm going to pretend it is, because he has brutal plans for me. Things no human should do to another.

"Be right back, baby."

"I am not your fucking baby! And where the hell are you going? You can't just leave me like this."

He storms back and leans over me. Grabbing my face in his hand, he smirks at me for a long minute before saying anything.

"I can, and will, do whatever I want to you."

A grin overtakes his mouth.

"There isn't a fucking thing you can do about it, baby."

I scream at his back while he walks out of the room, laughing.

Fuck, Bella. What the hell are you going to do?

Chapter Six
REAPER

I'm still laughing when I reach the garage. Her screaming at me was fucking beautiful, and I know it's going to get worse. She didn't want to be left alone. Living dead girl prefers my company over being on her own. She has an effect on me I did not expect. My cock has been hard as a rock, since I looked into her eyes as I killed the fucker who touched her shoulder. I have no problem getting an erection, but I don't normally get hard from simply looking into a woman's eyes. Usually, I'm far too busy choking the life out of them. I'm not planning to fuck her though, not yet anyway. I need to break her down a bit. Show her she doesn't have a fucking choice in anything. Her life is mine. Once she begins to understand, I'll let her make her choice. Be mine or die. If she takes option two, I'm prepared to kill her after I take her eyes.

Grabbing a bag, I pack the supplies I'll need. My drill, drill bits, chain, hitching ring, shackles, and a glass jar to fuck with her. I chuckle to myself as I add windshield wiper fluid to the jar, and put it in the bag, along with a hunting knife. Do I know I'm going to scare the fuck out of her? Oh yes, I do. In fact, I'm hoping she screams, cries, and attacks me, although fighting me is going to be a challenge, since she'll be chained to the wall.

I'm slightly out of my element, because I've never felt so drawn to a woman before. Not once before have I considered letting someone live. It was her eyes. They drew me in, and the thought of never seeing them again isn't a settling one. I know she won't like the options given, but there's really only one choice. I've learned through the years there is little a person won't do to save their life. Once I decide someone will die, from me choking the life out of them, it's done. There's no amount of begging or crying that will change the path. I've been offered money, information, and even fucking houses. I've never wanted anything other than death. *Until her.*

I zip up my black duffle bag, filled with everything I need, and head back to the house to play with my living dead girl.

"Fuck," I mutter under my breath when my phone starts ringing in my pocket. I pull it out and see Bones flash across the screen. Rolling my eyes, I answer with a huff.

"What?"

Immediately, he growls at me.

"Watch yourself, Reaper."

"You aren't my boss. Remember? You can order everyone around except for me. I'm busy. What the fuck do you want?"

I can picture him rubbing his temples, even though I can't see him. I know I have that effect on him.

"Let's try this again," Bones says with a long drawn-out sigh.

"Hello, Reaper. How are you, brother?"

I stand outside, staring at the house, itching to get inside. The tingling crawls down the base of my neck. The same one I get just before I end a life.

"I'll call you back later. I have a girl here."

"Alive or dead?" he questions me, and it's my turn to get annoyed.

"Fucking alive, alright. It's the girl from the cemetery."

I can imagine the look of disapproval on his face, but he doesn't say much.

"I need you in my office tomorrow, Reaper. And this is not a fucking request."

"Yeah, yeah," I respond and disconnect the call.

My brothers don't really have a problem with my extra-curricular activities, but Bones worries that I'm going to attract unwanted attention, and cause headaches for the family. There's pretty much nothing we can't get out of legally, but of course, he'd prefer to not

22

have to deal with it. I guess I don't blame him, because I kill easily, but still struggle with getting rid of the bodies. We are a close family, but I'm the black sheep. I know they don't approve of the things I do. Not because they're against killing people. That's something we all do, but because I'm drawn to it in a different way. Bones is known for breaking the majority of the bones in someone's body before killing them. Almost always, they have wronged him, in some way. That's the case for all my brothers, as it was for my father before he died. Although I have killed people for fucking with me or my family, that's not why I do it, generally. I like it. No, I fucking love it. I know there's something wrong with me, and that normal people don't do what I do. I went three years without taking a life. I fought the urge until it won out, and I couldn't refuse the compulsion for a second longer.

Walking inside, I go straight through the kitchen to the stairs, taking me back to the bedroom with my living dead girl. She sits cuffed to the bed, with pretty tears running down her face. The room is smaller than my room, and it's never really been decorated. It's got the same white walls, and light brown carpet, it had the day I bought this house. Placing my bag on the floor, I open it up and set all the items on the foot of the bed, while she watches me quietly. I put the jar, and hunting knife, on the dark-colored dresser beside the bed, and gaze at her wide eyes. Fuck. She's gorgeous. I can imagine her pounding heart in my own ears.

I pull my shirt over my head and toss it to the floor. Do I feel her eyes on my chest? Unfortunately, but I choose to ignore it, because my dick is straining against my zipper enough as it is.

I grab the drill, and attach my drill bit, before picking up the hitching ring and, using the lag bolt, I secure it to the wall. After I fasten the chain to it, she finally speaks.

"What are you doing?"

I don't respond. Instead, I keep working until I finish the job. Once I'm done, I place my drill back in my bag before removing her handcuffs.

"Thank you," she says as she rubs her wrists.

I shake my head at her while I laugh.

"Don't thank me yet, living dead girl."

She jumps onto her knees, and shoves me in the chest, with a glare in those pretty eyes.

"Stop fucking calling me that. My name is Bella."

I grab a fistful of her hair and yank her down onto her back. Leaning over her, I press my face to her neck, and inhale the scent of her skin. Fuck. If I have to kill her, I might need to keep that too.

"I will call you whatever I feel like, baby. You hold zero power here. The sooner you get it through your head, the better off you'll be."

Letting go of her hair, I move my hand to her throat and squeeze. Her eyes widen in response and the tingling is back. Like a separate physical force in this room. Real and visceral, the need to kill her is strong, and I don't know if I can fight it.

I want to keep her, but I also want to watch her die.

Grabbing her hair again, I pull her off the bed with me, while she screams and tears once again spring to her eyes. Dragging her to the wall, I shove her to the floor. She lays there helplessly, her beautiful gaze on mine, as I hold her down with my foot on her chest.

"Hold still, or I will cut your fucking eyeballs out right now, and end you."

Her breaths come out heavy and harsh, I can feel them on my bare foot, and fuck, it gets my dick so hard. Pulling the shackle from the floor, I motion for her arm and she gives it to me willingly. I'm not completely delusional. I do know if she had a choice, she'd be on her feet running from me. Again.

Once I have the one restrained, I nod for her other and do the same. I remove my foot from her, and she scrambles up with her back to the wall. Her blonde hair is a mess, blue eyes wide with panic, cheeks flushed, and her chest rises and falls quickly with shallow breaths. She couldn't look more alluring than she does right now if she tried. I squat down in front of her, taking in every fucking gorgeous feature. Too many to count.

She reaches up with one of her shackled wrists, and brushes her messy hair from her face.

"You have enough length to go to the bathroom, and even look out the window, if you choose to view the outside world through bars. You won't get further than that. As bad as you might think things are right now, don't fuck with me, baby. Things can, and will, get a lot worse."

"I understand," she says, but clearly she doesn't, because in her very next breath, she swings her arms up and wraps the chain around my throat, pulling as tight as she's probably capable of. I smile as she cuts off my air, because how fucking beautiful is this?

Chapter Seven
BELLA

"Harder," he says with a hoarse voice.

Harder? He is certifiably insane. That is not a normal reaction to someone pulling a chain against your throat, and trying to kill you to save themself.

The fact that he says it with a damn smile on his face should be even more terrifying, yet I find it intriguing. I'll admit, I watch a lot of serial killer documentaries. The minds of the corrupt and evil have always interested me. Right now is not the time for curiosity. It's the time to kill this asshole before he kills me, so I push it all aside and grip the chain on either side and pull harder. His eyes darken, and he wraps both his hands around my throat, and pushes me onto the floor. My hands slipped away from the chain when he moved me, but it still sits around his neck. He grins at me like the psycho he clearly is.

"Change of plans, baby. I'm going to fuck you, and then I'll kill you."

He keeps one hand on my throat, my thighs between his legs, and with his free hand, yanks open my shirt while I buck my hips up, trying to throw him off of me.

Chuckling, he says, "Yes. Fucking fight me."

I place both hands on his chest, and try to push him forcefully, but he's like a boulder. Unmoveable.

He pulls my bra down, exposing one of my breasts, and leans forward, biting my nipple hard, and causing me to scream in pain.

Using his knee, he separates my legs and pulls my skirt up, before undoing his pants and pulling out his cock.

"Nico! Don't. Please."

I try to hold the tears back, because if anything, my crying will only add to his excitement. I'm not normally much of a crier, so it infuriates me. Suddenly, I know I was right, because he stares at the wetness on my cheeks like it's a thing of beauty. His smirk turns into a wide grin.

Like anything else, he doesn't care. Everything I do or say to prevent this only makes him laugh.

I don't know if it's lack of experience, or because he wants to hurt me, but he pulls my panties to the side and pushes into me forcefully, in one-single thrust.

"Fuck," he groans.

"I wondered that night at the graveyard what you would feel like. This is better than I imagined. This pussy feels like life and death. I want you to live, so I can use it again and again. And I would gladly die right here."

"Please kill me," I beg him, as he rocks into me.

"Come for me."

He pulls his hips back and thrusts into me, over and over. Each time I want to die a little more than the time before. Nico, Reaper, whatever he wants to call himself, disgusts me. His sweaty body over mine, ordering me to orgasm while he takes something he has no right to, brings me back to my childhood, and I'd rather be dead than to endure this. And yet, as he leans down and presses his lips to mine, my body obeys him. He groans as my back arches from the floor, and I feel my pussy squeezing his cock. He pulls back from our kiss and stares into my eyes, and I hate myself. I hate myself for giving him everything he wanted. Everything he doesn't fucking deserve.

"Eyes on mine."

I do as he says, even though I really want to squeeze my eyes shut, simply to take this one thing away from him.

Slamming into me one final time, he groans as he releases inside me. His eyes get darker, as the pleasure is evident in his expression.

Pressing his hand to my face, his breathing is heavy, as he admits, "That was everything. I'm sorry I didn't last longer. I promise it'll get better."

What? That's not happening again.

"Kill me, Nico. Please. Take my goddamn eyeballs. Whatever you want. Just end my life."

He stares at me, with a tilted head and a look of confusion. Pulling out of me, he tucks himself back into his pants.

"You want me to kill you?"

I pull my skirt down and sit up, as I try to cover my exposed breast.

"Yes. I would rather die than experience that ever again."

His perplexed expression only makes things worse. He appears genuinely confused by my words, like he somehow thought I wanted that.

"That was amazing. I don't understand."

I shake my head in disbelief, because it's ridiculous that he needs this to be explained to him.

"You raped me, Reaper. Congratulations, now you're a rapist, as well as a murderer."

Glancing up, I spot the sad look on his face, and instantly hate myself again for feeling an ounce of sympathy for this delusional asshole.

"No. I didn't rape you. Maybe at first, but you liked it. You had an orgasm."

Things are bad enough being chained to the damn wall, but now I'm getting a migraine. Nobody is this fucking stupid. He has to know what he did to me.

"Just because my body reacted, against the will of my heart and mind, does not mean I wanted that. I hope you remember losing your virginity for the rest of your life. May you never forget how much you disgust me. I hate spiders, but I'd rather have a thousand of them crawling on me, than to ever have you inside me again."

29

He stands, staring at me for the longest time before he finally speaks.

"I'll be back later. If I stay here, I'm going to kill you, and I think I might regret it."

Reaper walks out the door and slams it behind him. I scream at the closed door like a banshee.

"Dick!"

The sound of a motorcycle rumbles outside, and I get up and look through the bars, and watch him as he drives away. Once he disappears from my view, the house is eerily quiet. Since I was a little girl, I couldn't stand the sound of silence. I always needed the tv or music on for background noise. This creeps me out, and every sound of the wind blowing outside the window causes me to jump. Now, I can't decide if I'm worse off alone in this house, or with a psychopath in front of me. I glance at the jar on the dresser. A chill runs down my spine at the mere thought of him cutting my eyes out. Chances are good that's going to be the end result. If I've learned anything about Nico Bonetti, it's that he gets what he wants, and fuck everybody else.

Chapter Eight

REAPER

May you never forget how much you disgust me.

I shake my head as I speed down the road to my club. Fuck her. *I should've killed her.*

The last thing I need is yet another person reminding me how abnormal I am. Do they really think I don't fucking know that? I know. I'm not the fucking idiot they all think I am.

'What do you mean, you get a tingling feeling in your neck?'

'We kill when we need to, not because we have a fucking bizarre urge.'

'How does walking the earth, killing people for no reason, benefit the family?'

My dad was the first to point out how different I am, and he's the one person that knew the real reason why. Where the rage stems from. Understanding why didn't matter to him, only that I was conducting myself in a way that did not benefit the Bonetti line. If it didn't make him money, or give him power, he didn't give a fuck. I'm close with my brothers, but they don't get me either. Nobody does.

And now, Bella is just like them. Maybe worse, because nobody in my family hates me, but she does. I'm not a fucking rapist.

There's a good chance I hate Arabella, if for no other reason than she makes me feel something. What, I don't know, but I don't like to fucking feel. It makes me so angry I can't fucking see straight.

Pulling up to the club, I spot a car in my parking spot. I'll deal with that in a moment. I dial my brother Kage, because I need to see him.

"Where are you?" I ask as soon as he answers.

"In your club, getting my dick sucked."

After hanging up, I park beside the spot stealer. I know the car well. *Alonzo Abruzzo.* Son of Vincenzo Abruzzo, a rival family, which makes me wonder why he's in my fucking club. Rival families are allowed here if they choose to be, sans weapons, of course. Only Bonettis can enter my club with any. I climb off my bike as I spot him walking to his car, and approach him.

"Is the fucking *no parking* sign invisible to you, asshole?"

He turns to me with a smug expression.

"I park where I want."

Narrowing my gaze at him, I say, "You used to park wherever you wanted. Back when you were alive."

Shrugging like it means nothing, he quips, "We all know you're a psychopath, Reaper, but even you aren't going to kill someone over a parking spot."

On any other day, he might be right, but today is not any other day, and he picked the wrong time to fuck around and find out. The familiar tingle travels down the base of my neck, and he recognizes the glint in my eye that people talk about. He knows when the sun rises, he won't be around to see it.

"Reaper. Come on, man. It's a fucking parking spot."

I step closer to him, and he reaches behind him, clearly going for his gun. I don't fucking think so. For a moment, I wonder if he was in my establishment with a firearm. I'll deal with my security shortly. After this asshole is dead.

Grabbing his reaching arm, I pull it up behind his back until he lands face down on the hood of his car, likely causing a dent. I smile sadistically at him as I flip him to his back, and wrap my hands around his throat and squeeze, while staring into his wide, panic-stricken eyes. He attempts to push me off him as he struggles to breathe. They always do. The will to live is one that intrigues me. Even people with shitty fucking lives will do anything to prolong their existence. A person will have nothing to live for, and still struggle to survive. It's fascinating.

And there it is. His eyes turn from a vibrant green to a glassy appearance. The one I enjoy so much. I don't know why. Bones says it's the power, but I'm not so sure. For me, I like the look in the eyes as they die. And it's the only thing that makes the tingling subside.

Letting go of him, I chuckle to myself.

Asshole.

I reach into his jacket pocket and find exactly what I need. Pulling the cap off his black sharpie, I write 'No' on his forehead, and 'parking' on his cheek.

After placing it in the pocket of my leather jacket, I walk into my club. Years ago, my father tossed me out of the family business, because he said I was a liability. A mafia war waiting to happen. He bought me this club as a parting gift, hoping it would keep me busy. It doesn't. There is someone for every job that needs to be done. Checking in weekly is the only requirement for me, to make sure everyone is doing what they're supposed to.

Walking inside, I nod to my doorman and step into the club. There are blue lights at the top of the ceiling, shining down to the black-tiled floor. The walls are black as well, but the lights make them look blue.

There's a large black 'U' shaped bar to my right, and I nod to my bartender that's working tonight; a pretty redhead wearing leather pants, and a matching sleeveless top. I keep walking through the gyrating bodies to the spiral staircase, and make my way to the VIP room, where Kage is likely getting his blowjob. I'm hoping he's done, but with him you never know.

When I enter, I spot a blonde on her knees with his dick in her mouth. I glance away while he finishes, but can't help but wonder how it feels. I know fucking feels amazing, but this I haven't experienced yet. I'm fairly confident, at this point, my living dead girl is not going to be into it. She's pretty pissed at me. Fuck, that confuses me because she had an orgasm. That had to mean that she enjoyed it, at least a little.

I tune out the sound of my brother's grunt, and stay turned away from him, until I hear him dismissing the girl. When I notice she's one of my waitresses, I roll my eyes and narrow my gaze at Kage.

"Is that why you come here? To get your dick sucked by my staff?"

He chuckles as he zips up his pants.

"You should try it. After all, they are here to serve you."

Not exactly. They are here to serve my customers. Besides, I only want Bella's lips wrapped around my cock. Even though, at this moment, I'd be concerned that she'd bite it off.

I take a seat beside him and motion to the waitress to bring me a drink. They all know my drink is whiskey, so I won't have to even give any instructions.

Miranda comes over and places a glass in front of me, along with a bottle of *Buchanan's 18 Special Reserve.* I pour myself two fingers, and Kage questions me.

"You look off. What's going on? Is there a body?"

I shake my head no, even though there most definitely *is* a body outside my club.

"Remember when Bones told you about 'Living Dead Girl'?"

He chuckles. "Yeah. The one that got away."

I throw back my drink and pour myself more.

"She's currently chained up in my house, but she's fucking with my head. I fucked her. She said it was rape. *But she came.*"

Kage arches an eyebrow at me with obvious surprise.

"You fucked her? Seriously?"

I glare at him and say, "Yes, I fucked her. That's not the point. Can you fucking focus?"

He chuckles softly, as he pours himself some of my expensive whiskey.

"I'm just impressed. That's probably the most normal thing you've done since you were a kid."

34

Taking a gulp of his drink, he swallows and says, "If you're looking for chick advice, you are barking up the wrong tree. I know nothing about them, except I like to fuck them."

That's helpful.

"Look, we are Bonetti men. We take what we want. Let her cry. She will get over it."

He shrugs. "If you want actual advice, you should talk to Bones. He has a wife now, so he probably knows more than I do."

I shake my head. "I'm good. He's going to be pissed at me as it is."

"Reaper. What did you do?"

Glancing around the room, I watch the waitress working the bar up here. There are only a few men at the bar, because you have to be approved to get up here.

"Reaper," he growls, as he clearly gets impatient with me.

"I might have just killed Abruzzo's son in the parking lot."

My gaze moves to my brother, as I stare at the shock on his face. "Why?"

I shrug like I don't know, even though I really do.

"He took my parking spot."

"Jesus Christ, Reaper. You're starting a mafia war over a parking spot?"

Chapter Nine
BELLA

I already sit terrified when I hear the motorcycle rumbling but then it suddenly stops. Taking a deep breath, I attempt to prepare for whatever the hell this nutcase has planned for me next.

"Honey, I'm home!" he yells as he walks up the stairs.

He enters the room, and I stare at the glass jar in his hand.

"I missed you, baby." He grins with a psychotic look on his face.

Reaper steps closer to me and leans over me, holding the jar in front of my face.

"You see, living dead girl, I think you were bluffing before. I thought to myself, would she really rather have spiders crawling on her, than to have my dick inside her? Then I realized, there's only one way to find out."

My heart pounds as he loosens the lid.

"Beg for my cock and I'll put my friends away."

"Nico," I warn, as my eyes feel like they might pop out of my sockets.

Instead of looking regretful, he looks pleased with himself. He stands beside the bed with a stupid grin on his face that makes my skin crawl.

"You really do have a fear of spiders. I bet you regret telling me how much I disgust you now. Don't you?"

Tears fall down my cheeks, but I don't respond because I can't breathe. Or move. I'm immobile in my state of panic, as he pulls the lid off the jar. I try to scramble backward, but there's nowhere to go. No way for me to avoid this.

Taking a spider out, he places it on my chest as he speaks softly.

"He isn't venomous. But that's not where the fear comes from, is it?"

I watch in terror, my body trembling as he takes out another spider, and holds it in his hand in front of my face. The sobs are instant, but I still can't move as much as I want to. The feeling of the first spider crawling on my skin causes panic to rise, as my body shakes uncontrollably.

He chuckles loudly. "You might want to close your lips. It would be terrible to have one crawl into your mouth."

The sensation of the spider crawling on me, and the sight of the one in front of my face, makes me want to peel out of my skin.

"Nico."

He runs his fingers through my hair, and leans down and swipes his tongue over the wetness on my cheeks with a groan. His hand in my hair is gentle, and it would be comforting if it were any other man. Yet with him, it's the complete opposite of soothing.

"You know how to make this stop, baby."

As much as I want to show him no weakness, I can't hide my fear. It's on display no matter what I do. And it's exactly what he wants.

"Why are you being so cruel? What did I do to you?"

He gazes into my eyes, and stares at me deadpan.

"I'm not being cruel. This is the nice version of me. Living dead girl, this is as good as it gets."

That might be more terrifying than spiders crawling on me. The one from my chest moves to my neck, and I've reached my breaking point.

"Do whatever you want to me, just put the goddamn spiders away. I'll do anything you ask."

Instead of putting the spiders away, he moves the one in his hand closer to my face.

"Convince me that you want to suck my cock."

I lie through my teeth.

"I want to suck your cock, Nico. Please put them away, so I can wrap my lips around you."

He arches an eyebrow in disbelief.

"Are you going to spit or swallow?"

"Swallow," I answer quickly, "I want to taste your cum sliding down my throat."

"Fuck," he groans and puts the spiders back in the jar. He places them on the dresser beside what I've decided is eyeball liquid.

"I'm going to leave them here as a reminder for you."

He stands to the side of the bed, and reaches back and pulls his black t-shirt over his head, before dropping it to the floor. His eyes never leave mine, as he unzips his jeans and removes them, along with his underwear and socks. Standing beside me, he strokes himself with a heated expression on his face. I hate that I even like his body. All his muscles on display should do nothing to me. If he wasn't such a cruel asshole, I might even want him. But I don't. I want no part of this. I just can't handle spiders on my skin. As much as I hate this man, he's my choice between bad and worse.

Climbing onto the bed, he places a leg on either side of my head, and once again strokes his cock, but this time he does it so my lips touch the tip.

"I want to be very clear, living dead girl. If you fucking bite me, you will become dead girl very quickly."

It's as if he read my mind, because there's nothing I'd like to do more than bite down until he bleeds. I want to be cruel to him. If I ever get the chance, I will hurt him in a way he has never experienced before.

Moving back slightly, he yanks my bra down, exposing both of my breasts to him. He stares at me like he's never seen them before.

"Beautiful," he says, his voice coming out low and almost sounding mesmerized.

"They're just tits."

He shakes his head. "No part of you is just anything, Bella. All the others I killed easily. No second thoughts. I never wanted them this way. Only you. Open your mouth."

"This would be far more pleasurable without chains."

Reaper gazes down at me, with a smirk on his annoyingly perfect lips.

"If only I could trust you, which I can't. Now open your fucking mouth."

I part my lips, and he shoves his cock into my mouth, until the tip hits the back of my throat. He groans when I gag slightly, which tells me there will be no mercy with this blow job, not that I expected there would be. He places his hands on the wall above my head, and pulls out of my mouth most of the way before sliding back in.

"Suck," he orders, so I hollow my cheeks and suck him, hoping I can hurt him with suction. It has the opposite effect, unfortunately.

He grunts loudly. "Fuck. Yes. Jesus Christ, baby. You suck me so well."

I whimper as tears run down my face.

Pulling his hips back, he slams into my mouth with such force it nearly knocks the air out of my lungs. Nico comes down my throat, and I pretend to not notice how sexy he is when all of his muscles tense up, and extreme pleasure shows in his face. He looks different like this. Less monster, more man. That all goes away when I spot the eyeball tattoos on his shoulder, and remember what he plans to do to me.

Chapter Ten
REAPER

I pull out of her mouth and lie down beside her, and she tries to fight me when I attempt to hold her.

"God damn it, living dead girl."

Grabbing her forcefully, I pull her against my chest, the chain and shackles digging into my skin, but I don't mind it nearly as much as she probably does.

"That was consensual. You asked me for it."

She rolls her pretty eyes at me, and mutters under her breath.

"Sure it was."

Bella is quiet and tense, almost like she has no control over her body.

"I want you to be mine."

She pulls her head back, and stares at me like I've lost my mind, and sighs loudly.

"Nico, just kill me. Get it over with. Please."

Once again, she's asking for death, and it does two things. It confuses the hell out of me and fucks with my plan. If I give her the choice between being mine or dying, will she choose death?

"Before, you wanted to live, but now you wish to be dead?"

"Yes."

I gaze into her beautiful eyes, and imagine a world where they don't exist. Hers are different from the many I've seen before. They don't only cause the tingling in my neck, they hold something I've never recognized before. Light. My world is dark. The brightest it gets is a dark gray. She's like heaven. Some place I'll never go. My living dead girl might be my only chance to experience the light. I'm aware that I'm like Satan breaking into heaven after he has been cast out. I don't deserve her glow, but that doesn't make me desire it any less.

Running my fingers down her cheek, I lie to her.

"If I kill you, I have to cut your eyes out first. Losing them isn't an option for me."

The most beautiful tears run down her cheeks.

"Is there anything you can give me first?"

I shake my head in confusion.

"What?"

"For the pain. I'm pretty sure that's going to be excruciating."

"I don't have any drugs," I lie again.

She nods. "Alright. No drugs then."

The pain in my chest is intense and immediate. Am I so repulsive, that she'd choose brutal pain and death over being mine? I know I'm not a good man, but I never thought I was this bad. I've never been good enough for anyone. I knew I wasn't the choice she'd normally make, but I thought I was a better option than death. I guess I was wrong.

"Do it now, Nico."

The hurt turns to anger within seconds, and the fucking tingling is back with a vengeance. Rolling her onto her back, and hovering over her, I wrap my hand around her throat and grit through my teeth.

"It would be so fucking easy to end your pathetic existence right fucking now."

Her beautiful eyes widen, as fresh tears fall, and her bottom lip quivers.

"You are not in control of anything. If you die, I decide when it's time, not you. Stop fucking begging me to kill you, because I'm not going to let you go until I'm ready to do so."

I keep my hand on her throat, but I'm not taking her air, as much as the urge is there.

"If I could go back in time, I would poison your coffee."

Lowering my head, I bite her bottom lip, causing her to whimper.

"You would poison me, baby?"

"In a fucking heartbeat," she says, with a glare that makes my dick hard all over again. Sliding my hand into her hair, I wrap it around my fist and pull, until she cries out.

"That's unfortunate for you. You will never get the chance again."

"Why are you doing this to me?" She sobs loudly.

"Because I can. You are mine. I own you now. It doesn't matter how loud you cry. If I want to fuck you, I will. If I want to decorate you with goddamn spiders, I will. If I want to lead you around on a collar and leash, I will. Any free will you once had is gone."

She spits on my face and screams at me. "I fucking hate you."

I wrap my hand around her throat again, and squeeze lightly. The way her pulse pounds against my hand nearly drives me insane.

"Lick it up."

She narrows her gaze, so I squeeze her throat tighter, and she sticks her tongue out. I lower my head, so she can get it all.

Letting go of her throat, I say, "Now it's time for you to be punished."

"No spiders," she sobs so loud it almost breaks my heart.

Then I remember I don't fucking have one. If I did, I wouldn't be able to snuff out lives as easily as I do.

I get off the bed and grab my hunting knife. Holding it pointed at her, I ask her a simple question.

"Who's in charge here, living dead girl?"

All I get from her is a glare, that causes a thrill to run through my body. She's a fighter, just like I wanted her to be. I don't want a limp body that won't push me. Even so, if she doesn't behave, she will be punished.

"I suggest you answer my question."

Rolling her eyes at me, she nearly growls, "You are, dickhead."

Jesus Christ. If she were any more perfect for me, I might start believing in God.

Gripping the center of her bra in my hand, I pull it away from her body, and cut down the center, finally exposing her entire stunning set of tits to me.

I grab the top of her skirt and do the same.

"You don't know much about me, baby, but I have these urges and they are difficult to control. Sometimes impossible. Right now, I want to cut you so bad it hurts. I generally prefer what they call a silent kill. There's no blood, but I can't stop wondering what yours would look like. Taste like."

Her eyes widen in response, as more tears fall from her flawless eyes.

"Please, Nico. I'm sorry. Please don't cut me."

Pulling her panties away from her skin, I take the knife and cut them off.

"I'll tell you what. If you take your punishment like a good girl, I'll do my best to control the urge to make you bleed."

Her trembling naked body is a fucking wet dream. I've seen naked women before, but nothing like this.

"Spread your legs, baby. I want to see my property."

The quiver in her bottom lip causes a thrill to shoot through me. I'm an animal for this woman, and her fear is the greatest fucking drug I've ever known.

"Please put the knife away, Nico. You're scaring me."

So my sassy, living dead girl does have fears. Spiders and knives.

I place it on the bed beside her, but out of her reach, because I'm not an idiot. She is chained to the wall. She can't run away, but she could grab the knife and kill me. With my beautiful girl, I know that is a definite possibility.

"We're going to leave it within my reach, Bella. Let's call it motivation."

Chapter Eleven

BELLA

When I squeeze my legs shut tight, he glares at me.

"Goddamn it. Spread your fucking legs, before I go buy a spreader bar, and your legs will be open twenty-four seven."

I don't have a clue what he's talking about, but we both know I don't have a say in the matter, so I do what he wants. It's always about what he wants.

He kneels between my legs and stares at my pussy like it's mesmerizing. The same way someone might gaze at a painting that makes them experience strong emotions.

Pushing two fingers inside me, he groans as he moves them in and out slowly.

"If I make you come, which of us will you hate more, baby?"

"Myself, but I'm not going to."

Chuckling as he leans his head down, he glances up at me with a stern expression.

"Good. This is for me. In fact, if you come, you get to choose the knife or a spider."

I whimper at the mention of either option, because both are equally terrifying. My childhood home had more spiderwebs than I would've ever thought possible. More than once, I woke up to spiders crawling on me. Before I moved out, I had been bitten so many times, I lost count. There's no real reason the knife scares me, other than I don't think anybody wants to be cut.

He continues fucking me with his fingers, and then swipes his tongue across my clit, instantly making me whimper with need I don't want. I don't want it to feel good. My hatred for him grows as quickly as my orgasm does.

"Reaper. Stop. Fucking stop. I don't want this."

He chuckles as he gazes up at my body.

"Too bad, baby."

Pulling his fingers out, he holds them up for me to see.

"Look how wet you are. You don't *want* to want this, but you do. Your sweet little pussy can't get enough of me."

"I fucking hate you. I hope *Dahmer* finds you and kills you."

Nico stops what he's doing, and looks into my face with pure amusement.

"He's dead, baby."

I scream, "Fine. *Gacy*."

Tilting his head to the side, he chuckles.

"Also dead. We need to work on your knowledge of serial killers."

I know he thinks he's funny, but he's wrong. He's fucking infuriating. Whatever serial killer is alive, I hope they come and end his life in the most painful way possible. Or maybe he'll walk outside someday soon, and a giant boulder will fall on his head.

He pushes his tongue inside me with a groan before he swirls it around. I buck my hips as he fucks me with it, and try to stop, but I can't. Grabbing his head by his hair, I try to pull him off me, but I can't. This shouldn't feel good, not with him. Looking down and seeing his face between my legs should repulse me. So why does it turn me on? Someone needs to remind my needy pussy that we hate him. He pulls his tongue back, and growls as he looks up at my face.

"Fuck. You taste incredible."

I roll my eyes and say, "I'm glad you're done."

Reaper chuckles softly.

"Not even close. This pussy has become my greatest obsession, and I may never finish drinking from it."

He runs his hands up the inside of my legs and digs his fingers into my skin.

"You will learn to like this."

46

A groan escapes from his chest as he takes a long swipe up my slit. I really wish it didn't feel like it does. I have two very good reasons not to orgasm, and I know the second he swirls his tongue over my clit that I'm done.

"Goddamn it, Nico!"

I'm frustrated because he was a fucking virgin, and he should not know how to use his tongue the way he does, unless he has experience. *Think about spiders and knives, Bella.*

Closing my eyes, I imagine hundreds of spiders crawling all over me.

He bites my clit hard, causing me to scream at him.

"Motherfucker!"

"Your eyes belong on me. Watch me eat your pretty pussy."

Lots of guys go down on women. In my experience it's to get whatever they want. Sex or a blow job. Not Nico. He licks me like he's going to literally devour me. As if there's nothing in the world he wants more. And we both know he doesn't have to do it to get what he wants, because he'll just take it anyway.

Placing his lips around my clit, he sucks it into his mouth, and I lose my mind. For a moment, I succumb to the pleasure, and forget how much I hate him, and what the consequences for this will be. The chain rattles as I move my hand to his hair and pull. The sound takes me back to the here and now, but it's too late. My body gives him exactly what he wants.

I scream out in pleasure, eliciting a groan from him that rumbles through my entire body. Pulling his hair harder as I tremble from head to toe, I scream at him.

"I fucking hate you."

He chuckles as he pulls away from my pussy.

"Haven't you heard, living dead girl? There's a fine line between love and hate."

Glaring at him, I say, "I may not be able to control my pathetic body, but I can control my heart. You can force me to orgasm, but I

47

will never love you. Hell, I won't ever even like you, you sadistic piece of shit."

Reaper grabs my hips, and flips me to my stomach.

"On your knees."

He squeezes my ass so hard it's painful.

"Words hurt, baby. You aren't being very nice to me."

"I doubt you have any feelings."

Stroking his fingers down my ass, he speaks so low I'm not sure I'm intended to hear it, but I do.

"That's what people think. Reaper is a psychotic asshole who feels nothing, but they are wrong. I fucking feel everything. Especially pain. There is no greater pain than going through life and never fitting in. It doesn't matter where you go, you're always out of place. It's a miserable existence."

Just as I begin to feel an ounce of anything other than hatred toward him, he smacks my ass hard. I yelp from the sting.

"Filthy fucking slut. You weren't supposed to come, but this pussy is ravenous and can't control itself."

He hits me again and again, each time harder than the one before. I'm a whimpering, sobbing mess, but not because he's really hurting me, but because even though I don't want to be, I'm turned on. He's going to figure out how wet I am, and it's only going to, once again, give him what he wants.

Pushing into me, he groans loudly.

"Fucking drenched. I don't care what you say, living dead girl. It's clear you want me to fuck you. You love being my whore."

I whimper as he leans over me and grabs the back of my neck, and holds my face down onto the mattress. He fucks me at a punishing pace while he pins me, so I can't move. All I can do is take what he gives me, and it's clear that he enjoys it. Gripping my neck in one hand, and my hip with his other, he slams into me repeatedly.

48

"Fuck, yes. I'm not going to kill you, baby. I'm going to keep you until I'm done using you, and then I'll end your life. Until I've had my fill of this pussy, you'll stay right here. It's not so bad though, is it? You love me using this beautiful body to get myself off. My pretty little fuck doll."

I hate myself so much. His words should make me sick to my stomach, not make me moan with pleasure. Instead of being bone dry like I should be, I scream out in an orgasm as he grunts his release inside me.

Pulling out of me, he moves to the head of the bed and plops down onto his back.

"Get over here."

He holds me against his chest, in what could look like a tender moment, but it's not. Through heavy breaths, he asks, "Did you decide between the knife and spiders?"

"No," I whisper, "Are you doing it now?"

Chuckling, Nico says, "No. We'll wait a bit. After all, the anticipation is the best part. I need a few hours of sleep before I meet with my brother."

I try to stay awake, so I can go to the foot of the bed and get the knife, and kill him while he sleeps, but once again my body betrays me at every turn. The warmth of his body pulls me into a deep sleep.

Chapter Twelve
REAPER

I wake up with the girl who hates me wrapped around me, like she never wants to let me go. The chain from her arm digs into my side, but it's worth every ounce of pain, as I stare at her beautiful face, asleep and peaceful. If she could see herself now, she'd be so pissed at herself. I want to fuck her again and I would, asleep or not, but I have to see my brother. Bones was already agitated when I spoke with him on the phone. I could hear it, but now that he probably knows I killed the Abruzzo family's pride and joy, he's going to be downright pissed off. I can already hear him bitching at me.

Reaper, why are you always making messes I have to clean up?

Bella moans in her sleep, and any control I had snaps like a fine thread. Gently, I roll her to her back and climb over her. After nudging her thighs apart, I sink inside her, holding back my grunt so I don't wake her up. I don't know if all women feel like this, since I've never fucked anybody other than her, but I'm not sure I'll ever get used to how she feels on the inside.

I rock into her, and she moans in her sleep for me again. Without taking my eyes from her, I pick up my pace to get myself off. Her pussy squeezes my dick as she moves her arm and pinches her nipple as she cries out in orgasm. Fucking beautiful. Her eyes pop open, and the look of pure pleasure is replaced with one of anger, which is just as stunning.

"Look at you, living dead girl. Your pussy loves this dick, even when you're not awake."

"Have you no boundaries, Nico?"

Changing my angle slightly, I fuck her harder, hitting her clit with my pelvis on every thrust, and I nearly laugh at her needy little whimpers. She wants to hate this so much, but she doesn't. I press my body against hers, but not putting my weight on her, and kiss and bite her neck.

"You were wrapped around me like the needy little slut you are. I had to have you before I left."

Every time I bite her neck, she whimpers, but then it turns to a moan when I lick the pain away. I tug on her ear gently, as I pull out and push back inside her pussy. I speak low, directly into her ear.

"Everything does not need to be a fight, Bella. We both know I make you feel good. You don't have to love me, or even like me, for me to make you come."

She sobs underneath me, and her chest shakes against mine, and it should make me stop, but it doesn't.

"I didn't want any of this. You think you're entitled to sex without consent, and even to take someone's life away. You're not. This is wrong. And I'll never forgive you for doing this to me."

Supporting myself with my hand on the mattress beside her head, I stare into her teary eyes.

"I know I'm the villain in your story. I'm a monster, the bad guy. Probably the worst man you ever met. But I don't care. I couldn't not fuck you, even when you begged me not to touch you. Now that I've had you, I'll never get enough."

"You make me sick."

I smirk at her.

"And you make me hard, baby. So fucking hard."

Leaning my head down, I press my lips to hers, and she bites my bottom lip. I groan in pleasure, not pain, which I'm sure wasn't her goal, as I force my tongue into her mouth while I fuck her. Bella reaches up and smacks the side of my head with the chain, but I don't care. When she runs her fingers into my hair and pulls the strands, while kissing me back angrily, it's all worth it. This woman is everything I want her to be. The fight in her is intoxicating. Even the way she fights for control with our kiss.

52

Sliding my hand into her hair, I pull as hard as she pulls mine, as I speed up my thrusts, fucking her like I hate her as much as she hates me. I don't hate her. How can you possibly dislike something so beautiful? Something that feels like this? Impossible.

I pull back from our kiss, we're both breathing heavily, and that same beautiful glare remains focused on me.

"Good girl. Hate me while you come all over my cock."

She's fighting so hard to not orgasm, but I know the struggle is over, when her pussy clenches down on my length like it never wants to let me go. I pinch her nipple, and she cries out as she loses the battle, and gives in to me, pulling my orgasm from me instantly. I fill her with my cum and she nearly chants, "I hate you. I hate you. I hate you."

I chuckle, because it's herself she hates most.

Kissing her neck, I groan just below her ear.

"I have to go see my brother. I'll be back."

Climbing off her, I stare at her for a long moment, simply enjoying the view.

"Maybe I'll get lucky and he'll kill you."

I start getting dressed as I laugh at her. Bones will be pissed, but he's still my brother. Unfortunately for her, he would never take out one of his own family. Knock me on my ass? Maybe. Probably, but he'd never end my life.

"Are you really just going to leave me naked all the time?"

I nod slowly, as I pocket my knife, so I don't come back to any unpleasant surprises, like my own fucking knife in my back.

"I do prefer you that way, baby, but if you could learn to behave, I wouldn't feel the need to keep you naked and chained up. Something for you to think about. In fact, if I could trust you to not pull stupid shit, we wouldn't have to be inside all the time."

Leaning over her, I kiss her quickly before turning and leaving her, to go deal with my annoying brother.

"What the fuck were you thinking?" Bones asks, with his gaze narrowed at me.

I shrug.

"I guess I wasn't."

Bones sits behind his dark-colored desk, looking like he wants to strangle me, as I sit on the other side fucking with the Newton's Cradle in front of me. I hit one ball against the other, like I don't have a care in the world, and it only pisses him off more.

"Goddamn it, Nico. You started a mafia war over a parking spot. What the fuck is wrong with you?"

I sigh audibly, because it only took five seconds of his barrage before I was done and checked out of the conversation. I can count on one hand the number of times any of my brothers have called me Nico. That's how I know exactly how furious he is, but I don't really care. He will get over it. Eventually.

"I was upset, alright? And it was my parking spot. He knew that, and parked there anyway. I'm not going to roll over and play dead, because you have a wife and kid on the way."

He rubs his temples and takes a deep breath.

"What were you so upset about?"

I laugh uncomfortably.

"Living dead girl."

Bones arches an eyebrow.

"I assume she's dead now?"

Shaking my head, I can't help the grin that overtakes my face.

"No. I was going to, but I fucked her instead. She's mine now."

"Let me get this straight. You kidnap her, try to kill her, then she gets away, and you find her and kidnap her again, and now she's yours? Is she insane?"

Using my forearm, I hit the stupid balls on his desk, sending it crashing to the floor.

"Say what you want about me, but don't talk bad about Bella. She's as off limits as Athena is."

"Bella," he says quietly.

"She is not insane, and she's not quite on board yet, but she will be. Don't act like you're better than me, Bones. We all know what you did to Athena before. For fuck's sake, you forced her to marry you. I'm not doing that."

He holds his hands up.

"Look, I made mistakes. There are things I wish I could undo, but I can't. That was before I had all the information. You could learn from my mistakes, but I know you won't, so I don't know why I bother wasting my breath."

Finally, something we agree on.

"I'm sorry for causing you trouble with the Abruzzos. There's nothing I can do about it."

He glares at me.

"There's one thing."

I cock an eyebrow, waiting for him to explain what he's talking about.

"It's time you come to work for the family. You have," he waves his hand in the air, "*gifts,* and you could use something to focus on."

"Dad kicked me out a long time ago."

He chuckles softly.

"With good reason, Reaper. Still, I think we can harness that darkness within you, to serve our needs."

"Can I think about it?"

This time his laughter comes out loud, obnoxious, and annoying as hell.

"It's not an offer. It's a demand."

I rise out of my seat and say, "Fuck this."

"Nico, you did this. You started a war, and it will not be long until they retaliate. You put your family in danger, and now it's only right that you help clean up the mess."

I know he's right, but I walk out anyway, because I'm pissed at the situation. My brother knows me well, so he doesn't try to stop me. Once I clear my head, I can figure out how to handle things. Until then, all I've got is this fucking tingling in my neck.

Chapter Thirteen

BELLA

It's funny how the worst time in our life suddenly becomes a place we would revisit, to escape our current hell. I grew up just outside of Detroit, and my childhood was difficult at best. I saw and experienced things no child should, and I swore I'd never go back to that area, however, Reaper has me changing my tune.

I was raised by a single mother, in low income apartments. Cherry Vale, on the outside, looked like a nice place to live. It wasn't. Everyday on my walk to school, drug dealers would approach me offering 'free treats'. On the weekends, I would be locked out of the house, while mom did cocaine with her friends. At eight, I was terrified for her well-being, as well as my own. When I was a teenager, she met a man, married him, and is now a religious nut that enjoys highlighting my transgressions, but forgetting her own. After all, she went to confession, and was absolved of all her sins. I guarantee you, she has no idea I've been kidnapped by a deranged lunatic. It will likely take close to a year for her to even begin to wonder where I am. Yet if my brother disappeared, she'd have some kind of sick intuition, and know instantly.

I sit on the bed, naked, shackled to the damn wall, and get more pissed off by the minute. How fucking dare he think he can do this to me? Evidently, I have the worst luck in the world, to have attracted the attention of this nut by simply doing my job.

Wedging my thumb and finger into the one shackle, I pull to try to break it, but only accomplish breaking a nail. Moving close to the wall, I grab the chain and pull as hard as I can. It doesn't work, so I decide on a new tactic. I turn to the door and run, attempting to pull the chain away from the wall, but the ring connecting the shackles to the chain snaps. One and then the other. I smile to myself, because

I'm getting the fuck out of here. I can't leave naked, so I rifle through the dresser drawers, trying to find something I can wear. Grabbing a black t-shirt, I pull it over my head. Reaper is at least a foot taller than I am, and muscular, so the shirt falls nearly to my knees, covering me adequately.

After searching for my shoes everywhere, and being unable to find them, I give up on being able to cover my feet. I might be a little cold, but I'll deal with it. I'm not going to freeze to death. However, in sixty-degree weather, I will be uncomfortable. Yet, it'll still be better than Reaper doing whatever the fuck he wants with me, which is clearly keeping me chained up, and fucking me non stop. Had he approached me like a normal goddamn person, I would've been into him. If he didn't go on about my eyes, and try to kill me. Nico is hot as hell on the outside, but on the inside? He's a complete nut job. I can handle a little darkness in people. I've been around it my entire life, but he's not dark, he's pitch fucking black. The strange thing is, it's not even the serial killer thing. Definitely not normal, but it's more than that. The fact that he wanted to cut my eyeballs out, and keep them, is more than simply wanting to kill me. It's disturbing. Deranged. I know he killed at an early age, but I do wonder what damaged him so completely that this is what he turned into. I feel like there's more to his story. I'm curious, but not enough to stick around and find out.

Walking out of the bedroom, I head downstairs quickly, because I know he went to see his brother, but I don't know how long he'll be gone. I need to be out of here before he returns.

I race to the back door and open it slowly, as if that's going to help me if he's on the other side of it.

All I can see are trees and then more trees. Shit. I'm going to walk into a forest, and find God only knows what. Glancing to the left and then the right, I finally decide to go left, but I'm not sure it even matters what direction I go. Walking through the trees, I move as quietly as possible, in case he comes back. He left on his motorcycle, so I'm fairly confident I'd hear him pulling up to the house. Still, better safe than sorry.

After walking for what feels like more than an hour, I realize my biggest mistake. I should have looked for water to bring with me. I spot the moon through the edge of the treeline, and breathe a sigh of relief. Hopefully, this will take me to a road, and I can find a ride, and get the hell out of wherever I am. The grass turns to sand, and I stop and look around, the best I can at night, and take notice of a sign facing in the other direction. Walking over to it, I move around until I see, 'Lake Bonetti - Private Property'. Of course he has his own lake. Maybe this is what he does with the dead bodies. Hell, maybe this will one day be my final resting place. Cement blocks tied to my limbs, so I sink to the bottom. The mafia do that, right?

I hear someone behind me, and I do the exact opposite of what I should do. Instead of running for my damn life, I freeze. Like an idiot. Hands grip my forearms and spin me toward him. Glancing up, as my heart pounds like a machine gun, I look into a face that is not the man I expect, and breathe a sigh of relief.

The handsome man in front of me, with dirty blonde hair, blue eyes, and built as well as Nico, tilts his head at me and points out the obvious.

"You have shackles on your wrists."

Tears stream down my face. He's capable, and appears strong. I have no doubt he can save me from the Bonetti madman.

"I've been kidnapped. Please help me get away."

He nods in what appears to be agreement, but starts asking questions.

"Why are you on the Bonetti property?"

Pushing my hair out of my face, I try to explain as quickly as possible, because time is of the essence.

"Reaper Bonetti kidnapped me. He says I'm his, but I didn't want any of it. Can you help me or not? If you can't, I have to go."

59

The sinister grin that develops on his lips causes a chill to run down my bones.

"You're his, huh? We can make this work."

Chapter Fourteen

REAPER

The second she left that bedroom, I knew she was on the run. Of course, I was fairly confident she wouldn't escape, but for extra safety, there's a tracking monitor on the insides of both bracelets. With nothing left to say, I walked away from Bones, and followed her here to our lake. The only surprise was Abruzzo's oldest son standing in front of living dead girl, who looks fucking stunning in my t-shirt. I watch them from the treeline, curious as to what my girl is made of. Chances are pretty good she thinks he'll save her. He won't. The second her life is in danger, his is over. She sees something in him she doesn't like, and backs away slowly. For every step she takes closer to the lake, he walks forward. The panic in her eyes pisses me off, and makes me struggle to control myself. I love it when she's afraid.

For me. Only for me.

The fact that she's giving him something that belongs to me causes the tingle in my neck to work overtime. He backhands her across the face, she falls to the ground, and he climbs on top of her. I've seen enough. I begin to walk toward them when I see something that causes my chest to swell with pride. Bella is fighting back, hard. She punches him in the face, knees him in the balls, and somehow ends up on top of him. Her blonde hair is a mess, and her eyes are wide with fury. My beautiful woman looks like the goddamn angel of death. I walk up to them and place my foot on his chest, holding him down, and she glances up at me with an expression that's hard to read. I'm not sure if she's happy to see me, under the circumstances, or upset.

"Nico," she breathes.

Vincent Abruzzo tries to move his arms, but he can't do much with my foot crushing his heart. We both know if I put more pressure on him, he's in serious trouble.

"Wrap your hands around his throat, baby."

She shakes her head no. "I can't."

I narrow my gaze at her. "You can and you will. This man planned to kill you, to avenge his pathetic brother's life."

Before removing my foot from his chest, I pull my knife from my sheath, and warn him.

"Make a fucking move, and I'll cut your eyeballs out and feed them to you. You made a big mistake by targeting what's mine. Make another and I promise you, you'll live just long enough to regret it."

I smirk at him as he stares at me with a panic-stricken gaze, and he trembles beneath my living dead girl.

Walking behind her, I nudge the asshole's feet apart, as she sits on top of him with both hands around his throat. Glancing into his face, I nearly smile, because this fucking pathetic sack of shit is immobile with fear.

"Squeeze, Bella. Look into his eyes and squeeze the fucking life out of him."

Kneeling between his legs, I lift my shirt she's wearing, and run two fingers along the outside of her pussy. She's fucking drenched.

"Good girl. Fucking perfect girl. Let the darkness in, living dead girl. Don't fight it. I promise it'll feel good."

Unzipping my pants, I pull my cock out, grab her hips and lift her slightly, and sink into her with a groan.

"Do not let go of him. Squeeze tighter. Look into his eyes."

She whimpers as I fuck her, while I know she's watching his light fade. I was pretty sure I'd never let her go, but this has sealed the deal. Even if she doesn't realize it yet, she's my other half.

"He's dead," she breathes through heavy pants.

I take a fistful of her hair and pull her head back.

"Good girl. Now fucking come."

"Nico!" she screams as I rail her in the dead of night. This is the soundtrack of my dreams. Her drenched pussy taking my cock, the splashing of water from the lake, and our heavy breaths.

She makes a sound, some kind of a strangled scream, and it sends me straight into a frenzy I never want to come out of.

"Harder," she screams, and at this moment there's very little I wouldn't give her. She can have it all. Every fucking thing she wants is hers. Unless what she desires is to be away from me, because that's not something she'll ever be permitted to have.

She places her hands on Abruzzo's chest, holding herself up, which would never be allowed if he were still alive. Releasing her hair, I move my hand and wrap it around her throat, without squeezing. Her pulse skyrockets as she whimpers.

"Nico, don't."

That's the thing about people that say they're ready to die. They rarely are. I knew that, when she asked me to kill her and be done with it. Placing my free hand on her stomach to hold her in place, I move inside her with hard thrusts, as I bite the side of her neck.

"You're going to give me everything I want, living dead girl. There will be no holding back. I want it all. Even the fucking air you breathe."

She whimpers and trembles under my control. This is how it's supposed to be. I'm the only man who gets her fear. I slide in and out of her tight pussy as she shakes. Do I know she is terrified, because she thinks I might kill her now? Yes, but soon enough, she'll experience what I want her to. An earth shattering orgasm. I'm an expert in controlling how much breath a person gets, and I haven't made a mistake since I was twelve years old. She may be pissed later, but right now, that intense state of terror will heighten everything for her.

I squeeze my hand around her throat, and she grabs onto my flesh and claws at me, trying to force me to release her, but I don't. I tighten my grip slightly and when her pussy tightens around my cock, I let her go and she gasps for air, followed by a scream. The fucking way she screams, as she comes apart for me, is my new favorite sound. I've never heard anything more beautiful in my life. If I hear it a million fucking times, it still won't be enough.

Pulling her back tight against my chest, I hold her while I come inside her, my face pressed to her neck, and I inhale her scent while I come undone for her. The only god damn woman I've ever managed to not kill. My pretty little living dead girl that keeps trying to escape from me. I'm not sure how I'll prevent her from doing it again, but somehow I will. At some point, Bella will learn that fleeing is not an option. Every time she takes off, I'll find her again. There's nowhere too far. I will always find her. I don't care how angry it makes her. She doesn't realize yet that when she's pissed off, and acts nearly as unhinged as I am, it doesn't upset me, it fucking thrills me.

"I hate you even more now. You're such an asshole."

I sigh with satisfaction. My girl doesn't know what I do. She is just as fucking psychotic as I am.

Chapter Fifteen

Bella

He smirks at me.

"I believe you hate me, living dead girl. But I also know you love the way I fuck you."

Getting up, and away from whoever the hell this dead guy is, I glare at Reaper with all the hatred I feel for him, straight to the very core of my soul.

Climbing off his knees, he tucks himself back into his pants and charges for me, like the monster he is. Reaching up, he touches the side of my face tenderly, and I hate it. I hate that I like it. What's wrong with me? I'll never admit it to him, but I know the truth, and it makes me sick to my stomach.

Reaper lowers his face so it's close to mine, and speaks in a gravelly tone.

"Did he not deserve to die?"

I shake my head no.

"We don't get to decide who lives and dies. You are not God, Nico."

He barks out a laugh.

"Do you know what he would've done to you? Do you have any fucking clue?"

I cross my arms over my chest and shake my head again.

"Of course I don't know, because I never met that man in my life."

He narrows his gaze at me, before his face registers a pained expression.

"He would've started by raping you."

I roll my eyes at his stupidity.

"Well, that would be nothing new, would it?"

Nico places his thumb and forefinger on my chin, and lifts my head gently so my gaze is on his eyes, and a chill runs through my body. I'm unsure if it's because of the way he's staring at me, or the cool breeze blowing through my hair.

"I know you think that's what I did to you, Bella. It's not. Everything I've done to you would have been a walk in the park. He would have been brutal with you. And then he would have sliced you from head to toe. I would have found parts of your body scattered across my beach. He would have taken your eyes to punish me, but everything else would've been here. I know you think I'm wretched, but I promise you there are worse."

I can't help the gasp that escapes from my throat, because he paints a terrifying picture. Would that man have really hacked me up and spread my body parts on the beach?

"Who is he? Was he?" I correct myself.

"Vincent Abruzzo. I killed his baby brother, the golden child of their family. The Abruzzos are rivals. They've lost a lot of control over the past few years and have become desperate. The men in my family are not what you'd consider good men, Bella. The Abruzzos don't simply kill like I do for the thrill of it. They torture. What I am capable of doing to you pales in comparison."

I swallow hard, because someone worse than Reaper is hard to imagine, but his words come across as sincere and genuine. I believe him.

"Was there a reason you killed him?"

I already know Reaper kills to kill, but with him being from a rival family, I wonder if there's more to it, because it seems like you might be more careful with who you kill, if he comes from such a powerful bloodline.

He shrugs with a smirk on his lips.

"He took my parking spot."

"You're insane, unhinged, and completely reckless."

Reaper chuckles like he doesn't have a care in the world.

"Now you sound like my brother."

Narrowing his gaze at me, he reaches into his pocket and pulls out his cell phone as he instructs me, "I have to call my brother. Don't move. I will chase you. To the ends of the goddamn earth."

"Bones," he says, "Vincent Abruzzo is dead."

Of course, I can only hear his side of the conversation, but it doesn't take me long to gather that his brother isn't happy.

"Did you expect me to allow him to kill me instead? Would that be the easier outcome for you, Bones?"

Bones?

I file that away for later, because now is clearly not the time.

"Yeah, well, he took my fucking parking spot. That's disrespectful, Luca."

His jaw clenches, and I think this is the first time I've seen Nico really mad.

"Well, it's business, so I expect you to send someone to handle this corpse."

He balls his free hand into a fist, as his eyes darken while continuing to argue with his brother.

"What do you think I'm going to do, Bones? If he sends another, I'll kill him. If he sends one hundred, I'll kill every last one of them. He was going to hurt my girl to get to me. How would you react if it were Athena?"

"On the beach," he says before disconnecting the call.

"Let's go, we're going inside. Someone will be here to take care of this."

Leaning down, he lifts me into his arms.

"I don't want you to hurt your feet," he says, when I arch an eyebrow in surprise.

He winks at me, with a devious grin on his impossibly handsome face.

"Put your arms around me, baby."

I huff in annoyance, but hold on to the back of his neck and warn him.

"Don't try anything, Nico. I'm not fucking around."

He chuckles as he squeezes my ass.

"I'm going to feed my sexy little killer before I do anything."

There's no doubt that this crazy man thinks what I did is wonderful, but I don't agree. There's nothing okay with taking someone's life, even if they are a bad person. I hate what I did, and knowing I'll probably need to do it again doesn't sit well with me. It's becoming clear that death is the only way I'll ever get rid of Nico for more than a short time. He said he'd never let me go, and I'm beginning to believe him. I don't get what it is, but he seems obsessed with me. None of it makes sense to me because he's hot. He could easily find another crazy woman to kill through life with him, but I'm not her.

He walks, carrying me through the trees for what feels like hours, until I finally spot the lights in the house. Glancing around, I realize we are at the front of the house, as he carries me over the cobblestone around the massive fountain, and up the steps. He sets me down just inside the house, and I take in his stunning home.

The foyer is large, with red Spanish tile, and a giant crystal chandelier above my head, creating a soft glow over the area. As I follow him, we end up in a living room that feels too large to be called something so ordinary. It's bigger than my entire apartment. The floor is white tile, but I can tell by a simple glance that it's expensive. The walls are a moody looking blue, with a large painting of a little boy playing with a puppy. My eyes stay locked on the portrait, and it piques my curiosity, because it doesn't look like something I'd expect to find in his home.

He stands beside me when he notices where my attention is.

"That's me. My mom is a bit of an aesthete. We have a family friend that's an artist, and he did this one."

I resist the urge to touch the amazing picture, but say, "You looked so normal. Happy."

Turning to him, I watch him shrug, and he narrows his gaze at me.

"What's normal, living dead girl? And I am happy. You think, because I enjoy ending lives, that I'm living some kind of miserable existence? I have demons as much as the next guy, but I'm not unhappy."

While I hear the words coming out of his mouth, I still can't agree with him. There must be some deep seated reason he does the things he does. People aren't born into this world as serial killers. Something happens along the way, that shapes them into the evil creatures they are. I'm curious what his damage is, but I'm still more interested in getting away from him.

"Nico?"

He stares into my eyes like he is lost.

"Will you please let me go?"

He strokes his fingers down my cheek, causing a shiver to run down my spine.

"No. Never. Unless you kill me and, fuck, living dead girl, I hope you try."

"Psycho," I reply under my breath, which only makes him laugh again.

"That's my brother."

I arch an eyebrow in confusion and he explains.

"I have three brothers. Bones, Kage, and Psycho. We all get our nicknames from our way of handling things. Reaper is because I enjoy killing people. Bones likes to break the bones of his enemies. Kage likes to cage people like animals. Psycho is a complete, well, psycho. He is the oldest, but isn't the head of the family, because he can't or won't control himself. Like myself, he tends to bring unhinged chaos wherever he goes. Neither of us think things through like Bones does. We are quick to react to a situation, instead of

considering all the repercussions before making a move. That's my family. Tell me about yours."

Chapter Sixteen
REAPER

Taking her hand, I pull her into the kitchen with me and lift her onto the granite countertop. The need to have her right beside me at all times is strong, and instead of dissipating, it only grows. While I prefer her naked at all times, I have to admit to myself that she looks gorgeous, sitting in my house wearing my t-shirt. Her long blonde hair is a mess, and those blue eyes I'll never get enough of watching me, like at any moment I might attack her. Initially, I wanted to end her life, but now I want to protect her from any danger. I'll still cause her pain, but nobody gets to make her cry but me.

"Are you going to punish me?"

I ignore for the moment that she avoided my questions about her family, and answer her.

"No."

She breathes a sigh of relief before she asks, "You won't let me go, so does that mean you'll chain me up again?"

I shake my head as I begin grabbing food from the refrigerator.

"Bella, I don't know what to do with you. I'm nice, and give you enough length, so you can use the restroom and move around the room, and you run the first opportunity you have. Maybe my brother has it right. Perhaps you need to be in a cage, so there's no possibility of escape."

Heating the oil in the skillet, I add the beef strips, as she begs me.

"No. Please, Nico. I won't run. I promise. I'll behave."

Do I believe her? Not a fucking chance, but I also don't want to chain her up, or cage her. The chains didn't keep her here, anyway. They only slowed her down.

Taking the onions and green peppers to the counter, I slice them, while standing beside her.

"If you try to run again, I'll have no choice but to resort to drastic measures. Assuming you can actually behave yourself, I'll let you have some freedom."

"Thank you," she breathes.

"Can I help?"

Glancing at her, I ask, "Can I trust you with a knife?"

She nods as she hops off the counter.

"I'm not going to do anything, Nico. Certainly not tonight, because, honestly, I'm exhausted."

Walking across the kitchen to the sink, she washes her hands, as she looks at the matching stainless steel appliances.

"This place must have cost you a fortune."

"Mmmhmm," I hum. It most definitely did, but it was worth every penny.

She comes back over and cuts the onions, while I stir the meat. I don't trust her completely, so I glance at her frequently, to make sure I don't end up with the knife in my back.

"So your family," I ask.

I smirk at her when she rolls her eyes at me.

"I was an only child, and grew up with a single mother. We aren't close. It's complicated. As a kid, my mother's bedroom had a revolving door. There were drugs and a lot of partying. Then she met my step dad, and turned into a religious nut. Everything I do is never good enough. When I was fourteen, she had my brother. The golden child who does everything right, while I do everything wrong in her eyes. I spent years trying to earn her approval, but eventually I stopped seeking the unachievable."

Her words cause the tingle in my neck to come back, but I know it's not her, it's her mother. Bella has awoken something inside me, that makes me want to kill everyone who has ever hurt her. Sure, I'll kill without a reason, but this infuriates me. I need to do a background check on this mother of hers.

"I'm sorry. One of my biggest pet peeves is shitty parents. People like that shouldn't be alive."

Her eyes widen in response.

"I can't confide in you, if I have to fear you killing people, Nico."

Holding my hands up, I say, "I won't kill her."

It's a lie, but she relaxes. If I end her mother's life, I'll have to be more creative, and make it look like an accident.

Grabbing the vegetables, I pour them into the pan with the meat, and cook them.

She stands beside me, glancing at the food with excitement.

"That smells really good. I'm starving."

I grin and don't say anything, but I always work up an appetite with killing. I wonder if she'll be the same. Bella probably thinks tonight was a one-time thing, and that she won't kill another person. She's wrong. I saw her while she choked the life out of that fucker, and I felt how wet she was. Bella doesn't want to get aroused from taking a life, but she did. Eventually, she's going to need to face it, because the urge will not go away.

I grab the plate of food, and she follows me out to the dining room. Turning to her, I chuckle as I watch her glance around the room. She stares at the coat of arms for our family name hanging on the wall, before she takes a seat at the table. It's a large glass table with a gunmetal gray border around it. She runs her fingers around the smooth finish, as if she's inspecting it, before she takes her seat.

Setting the plate in the middle of the table, I narrow my gaze at her.

"If I go get us drinks, are you going to do anything stupid?"

She shakes her head no.

Sighing audibly, I say, "I don't want to treat you like a child."

Rolling her eyes at me, she complains.

"No, you want to treat me like a prisoner."

I run a hand through my hair and order her to stay put. It's not that I want to treat her as a prisoner. There never would've been shackles on her wrists had I not deemed it necessary. I will keep her, whether she likes it or not. However, I'd prefer her to like it or at least accept it.

I walk back into the dining room with two glasses, as well as a bottle of wine, and I'm relieved to find her sitting there like I told her to.

She tilts her head, with a sassy smirk on her beautiful lips.

"See. Still here, Nico. I should get a reward."

I chuckle as I pour us both a glass of red wine.

"And what kind of reward do you think you deserve for simply staying put?"

After I sit across from her, I take a sip of wine while I wait for her to answer my question.

She stares at me sweetly, but I can see she's nervous. She grabs her fingers with her other hand, pulling like she's afraid to tell me what she wants.

"Umm-"

Reaching across the table, I take her hand, and rub her trembling fingers.

"You can tell me what you want, baby. There's no guarantee you'll get it, but I'm not going to hurt you for saying what you want."

She glances down at the table and takes a deep breath.

"I'd like these shackles to be removed."

Shaking my head no, I say, "Sorry, but that's not going to happen."

I can't explain why, because I don't think she'd react well to being tracked, but I'm unwilling to risk her getting away, when I might not be able to find her.

She makes herself a fajita while I do the same, and we begin to eat. I know she's upset, because she hasn't looked at me once since I refused her request.

"Bella. Look at me."

Swallowing her food, she lifts her gaze to mine and for the first time ever, that pained expression bothers me, even though I know it shouldn't.

"I'm sorry you're unhappy."

"Are you though?"

I nod slowly.

"If I say it, I mean it. I'm not a good man, but I am an honest one."

Chapter Seventeen

BELLA

He's sorry I'm unhappy? That's the biggest crock of shit I've ever heard. Nico doesn't care if I'm miserable or not. I don't think he cares about anyone other than himself. He has proven that to me time and time again. And that is the reason Reaper Bonetti needs to die. I don't want to kill again, but to save myself, I will. For now, I'll play by his rules. Until he trusts me enough to relax enough for me to kill him. There will be no hesitation, because I know I will only get one chance. If I try, and fail, he will not let his guard down twice. In fact, he would probably kill me.

We finish eating dinner, and I go with him to the kitchen and help him clean up. It's strange, the way he moves in sync with me, as if even when his back is turned, he always knows exactly where I am. After he starts the dishwasher, he reaches behind him and grabs my arm, as he turns to face me and pulls me against his chest.

"Go into the living room and get comfortable. I have to make a phone call. Be a good girl, and I may have a surprise for you tomorrow."

I pull away from him and, as I walk to the other room, I feel the eyes of a predator on me, every step of the way. Taking a seat on the black leather sectional, I wait for him to come and join me. I hear him talking on the phone, but cannot understand what he's saying, because he keeps his voice low.

He walks into the room, and pulls his shirt over his head while he steps closer to me. My eyes immediately drop to his sculpted chest and arms, that tell me he must spend a lot of time working out. Nico sits on the sofa beside me and grabs my hips, turning me toward him, and my gaze immediately lands on his shoulder. I reach up and drag my fingers over the tattoo on his shoulder of an eyeball.

"Explain this."

Arching an eyebrow, he says, "Explain what? It's a tattoo."

Crossing my legs on the sofa, I hold my shirt down, so I'm not exposing anything.

"What's with the eye fascination?"

He stares into my eyes, but he looks far away and lost in his thoughts.

"The eyes display emotions. Fear. Sadness. Happiness. Anger. When a person dies, as you've now witnessed, they go from expressing the emotion they are feeling, usually fear, to nothing. Their eyes take on a glassy appearance, and frequently the pupils are dilated. I can't explain it, but it's captivating."

"Were you really going to cut my eyes out?"

He smirks at me, and suddenly seems to be out of his lost state as he focuses on me.

"You were the first person I've ever considered cutting them out of and keeping them. Your eyes are the most expressive I've ever seen. And the thought of never seeing them again physically hurts."

Shaking my head, I say, "That's not normal. In fact, it's the polar opposite. What's your damage, Nico Bonetti? Something happened to make you this way."

His face falls, before he quickly hides behind that handsome mask. Clenching his jaw, he grits through his teeth.

"I have been told all my life how fucked up I am. I do not need a reminder from you as well."

Sliding his hand into my hair, he winds the strands around his fist, and yanks my head back painfully.

"Now I want to punish you. Do you think I'm unaware that it's not normal? That I'm not fucking normal?"

The glare in his eyes is frightening. He yanks my hair harder and growls at me.

"You are the one person I wanted to accept me as I am, but you don't."

78

It's not his anger that catches me off guard, but the pure pain in his expression.

"I need to hurt you."

"Nico, I'm sorry," I whimper as the tears spring to my eyes. Not so much from the stinging in my head, but because, other than murder, I don't really know what he's capable of. I don't want to find out.

Rising off the couch, he leans down and lifts me over his shoulder.

"Where are we going?"

"Upstairs. I don't want to get blood on the sofa."

Chapter Eighteen

REAPER

I have two hours before Psycho gets here to have her ready, but drugging her now would be too easy. I need to hear her scream and she will, but I don't want to risk her not remembering what's about to happen.

Setting her on her feet, I order her, "Face down on the bed."

"Nico, please."

Shaking my head, I tell her, "Do as you're told. This is going to be bad enough for you, don't make it worse than it has to be."

Pulling her fist back, she punches me in the face, and I let her. I fucking love it when she fights me. I grin, which only makes her angrier as she looks to the door. Silly living dead girl should be more careful about giving away physical cues. As she attempts to dart past me, I grab her throat, stopping her in her tracks.

She stands in front of me, with tears streaming down her face, and it should probably make me change my mind about what I'm going to do to her. I should feel bad. Yet, I don't. I'm as fucked up as everybody says, just like she reminded me of tonight.

I point to the bed, and she turns with a huff and does what she's told. Removing my pants, I grab the knife from my sheath, before spreading her legs and climbing between them. Bella trembles with delicious fear, as her sobs grow louder in the otherwise quiet room. I pull her t-shirt up to the middle of her back, exposing her beautiful ass, and a groan slips out of me. I drag the tip of the knife over her ass, not cutting into her skin, but the way she cries, you would think I'm butchering her.

"You can love me or you can hate me, living dead girl. It makes no fucking difference to me. But you are mine. Mine to fuck and mine to torture. Think what you want of me, but you won't dare to speak to me with the disrespect you had for me earlier. I don't want to cut your tongue out, but I will."

"I'm s-s-sorry," she stammers pathetically.

Pressing one hand on her back, I hold her down, because she's going to fight, or at least try to.

I dig the knife into her ass, carving my first initial.

"N," I say out loud, while she screams obscenities at me.

"You fucking psychotic asshole."

I chuckle as I start the next letter. Making the cut, I say, "I," as the blood runs down her ass. Then I move to the other cheek, and cut into her stunning flesh.

"C," I say, as she screams so loud that if I had neighbors, I might be worried.

"I hate you. I fucking hate you."

One last time, I slice into her skin.

"O," I say, as I watch the way her flesh turns red from her blood. I toss the knife onto the side of the bed, lean down and taste her, the way I've always wanted to. Knives aren't my favorite. This is a trick directly from Psycho's book, but it works for me, so I did it.

"Your blood tastes almost as good as your pussy."

"Why are you doing this to me?" She shouts.

Pushing her shirt further up her back, I rub the blood all over her exposed skin, and slam inside her.

"Because I can, Bella. I can do whatever I want to you, and there isn't a fucking thing you can do about it. Cry as much as you want, it has no effect on me. Run, and I'll find you. I've told you before, you have no power here."

She sobs while I fuck her sweet pussy. Every thrust makes her cry louder, but it doesn't deter me. I wasn't going to do this to her. As much as I wanted to, I tried to hold my urges back, but then she did what they all do. She judged me and I knew she needed to be punished. I've marked her permanently, and no matter what she does, she's mine.

"So beautiful. Even more so, with my name carved into your ass."

"Fuck you," she screams back at me.

I dig my fingers into her cuts and fuck her harder, while she cries underneath me. Fucking perfection.

When I finish, I climb off her but she doesn't move.

I grab the syringe from the back pocket of my jeans, that I brought with me to the beach earlier, but was happy to not have had to use it. Now I do though. Pulling the cap off, I expose the needle, and walk over to her and brush the hair off her neck. Touching the needle to her neck, she freezes as I smile.

"Goodnight, baby."

"Nico. Don't. I'm sorry, okay? I don't want to die."

If I were a decent human being, I'd probably tell her I'm not killing her, just putting her to bed for the night, but I'm not, so I'm silent as I push the needle into her flesh, and give her the medication that will have her out for the entire night.

After throwing out the syringe, I grab my first aid kit and tend to her open wounds. I didn't cut deep, so I'm not worried about her bleeding out, but I do want to clean her up. Taking my time, I wash the blood from her skin, and cleanse my name on her ass. She looks good with my name on her. I stare at my handiwork for a long time as pride swells in my chest. 'Mine,' I say to myself.

Once I get dressed, I go downstairs after my brother messages me that he's here, with what I requested from him earlier. He comes in and eyes me suspiciously.

"Are you sure about this? It's a little more my style than yours."

I shrug my shoulders.

"She wants the shackles off, so this is the only other option."

He chuckles softly.

"Has it ever struck you that we are the most alike, and I'm the oldest while you're the youngest?"

We are all brothers, and close, but I have always known that I was more like Psycho than either Bones or Kage.

"Maybe the psychotic gene skipped the other two."

He arches an eyebrow in obvious disagreement.

"They do fucked up shit too, but not to the degree that we do. Can I meet her?"

I glare at my brother.

"No. She's naked and drugged. And you aren't seeing my woman without clothing."

"Your woman?" He asks with that familiar tilt to his head.

"My name carved into her ass says she is. Thanks for the device. I need to go implant this."

He nods slowly.

"Call me if you need help."

Once he leaves, I head back upstairs to implant the tracker into Bella's ass. It's going to hurt there anyway when she wakes up in the morning, so it makes sense to put it there, and it shouldn't raise any suspicions.

Chapter Nineteen

BELLA

Immediately upon opening my eyes, I whimper in pain. Everything hurts. My head is pounding, and makes thinking difficult, because my brain feels like it has been scrambled. My ass throbs like someone butchered me.

Oh my God.

Parts of my memory slam into me, and I remember crying while he held me down and cut his fucking name into my ass. Moving to get up, I'm quiet, because the asshole is sleeping on the other side of the bed. Part of me believes he did that because he's a psychopath, so of course he would, But the other wants to see something more to Reaper than there appears to be. I saw his anguished expression, when he thought I was judging him. He was right, he feels pain. It was clear as day. I wasn't trying to judge him, I was trying to understand him.

I spot the knife on the bedside table and then glance at him. He is still passed out. This might be my one chance to get away. Walking over as quietly as possible, I take it in my hand and turn to him. Staring at him, I tighten the grip on his weapon, and his eyes pop open and land right on me.

"Bella," he warns.

He rises to a sitting position and I panic.

"Don't fucking move, Nico."

Holding his hands up in the air, he admits what he thinks I want to hear.

"Look, baby. Last night, I probably went too far. I'll make it up to you."

I tilt my head at him as I stare at him with disbelief.

"Too far? You butchered my ass like you had a right. You have never had a right to do any of the things you've done to me. I never wanted to take a life. I'm not like you. All of this is everything I've never wanted. You said you would break me. Congratulations. I'm broken."

I stand here staring at him, contemplating whether or not I can kill him, and I know I can't. What I don't understand is why. He has given me every reason to end his life, yet, when I look at the pain in his eyes, I just can't.

Lifting the knife to my throat, I feel relief, because this is how it ends. This is the only way.

"Bella. Jesus fucking Christ. Put the knife down."

My hand holding the knife trembles, so I steady it with my other one and smile. Not because I'm happy. That's far from my current emotion, but because now I'll be free of him. There won't be any more torture. Never again, will I wonder how he will kill me, because I'll already be dead.

"This is the only way this ends. One of us needs to die."

"No!" He roars, and his voice comes out drenched with anguish.

"Bella, I'm an asshole. I know that. But, baby, please, you're the only good thing in my life. Please don't do this. I'm begging you. Don't do this to me."

Do this to him? I'm ending my life, and he's worried about how it will affect him. The anger rises and causes my blood to boil.

"Even now, it's all about what you want. You never think about anyone other than yourself."

Taking a deep breath, I'm ready to leave all this behind. I'm not suicidal, not really. I think most of us that choose death don't actually want to die. We just don't want to live like *this*.

"Goodbye, Nico."

Without warning, he jumps up from the bed, and grabs my arm holding the knife. My heart pounds furiously as I grip the handle tighter, and he attempts to yank it from my grasp. I push forward, and the blade plunges into his chest. A scream is trapped in my throat, as he falls to his knees before crumpling to the floor. I stare at the impaled blade, knowing full well it's near his heart. Nico is going to die, and I can't for the life of me understand why I care. Why the pain in my own chest matches his. My heart squeezes in anguish, as my gaze moves to his face.

With a smile, he grunts in pain.

"I knew you were special. The one woman stronger than all the men. I knew there was a reason I fell in love with you, living dead girl. Go. Live your life. Your purse is in the kitchen pantry."

Grabbing his phone, I ask for his passcode.

"3223."

His eyes close, and I look in his phonebook and find his brother Bones. That's the one I should call, right? He's in charge, so it seems right.

"Reaper," he says after answering almost immediately.

"Umm this is Bella. Nico has been stabbed. You need to come get him or he's going to die."

I disconnect the call and set the phone down and stare at him on the floor. Regret fills my stomach, as he says words he never would have, had I not plunged a weapon into his chest.

"Go, Bella. Before my brother gets here."

There is no way I should feel anything other than hatred for him, after what he has done to me, but if I'm honest with myself, I don't. After everything he has done to me, why won't my feet move? I should be running for my life, but I don't want to go. I run a hand through my hair and pull at the strands.

Nico speaks low, as if it hurts to talk.

"Go, baby. If I lose consciousness, I cannot guarantee your safety. Please leave."

I walk to the door, my legs as heavy as lead, as I walk away from the most psychotic man I've ever known. Tears stream down my face, as I realize I'm never going to see him again. My brain tells me I shouldn't care, but my heart says an entirely different thing.

My chest tightens as I make my way to the pantry to get my purse. I'm fairly certain if I'm here when his brothers show up, I'm dead. That's what he meant about not being able to guarantee my safety. I don't think I've ever heard of a member of the mafia sparing someone that killed one of their own.

Chapter Twenty

BELLA

One Week Later…

Life without Nico has been odd, to say the least. I imagined I'd go back to my life and things would be normal, but I don't know what normal is anymore. I'm kind of lost. I sit watching tv while I sip my coffee, when my world is rocked to its core. A special report breaks through the episode of some stupid sitcom I've been watching.

"We've just learned that Nico Bonetti, better known as Reaper, has been killed in his home. Nico was the son of the late Lorenzo Bonetti, former head of the Bonetti Family, and is survived by his brothers, his sister, and his mother, Lucia Bonetti. He died from stab wounds a week ago. No further details are available at this time, but we will keep you updated on any developments."

I killed him.

All the air escapes from my lungs, as the coffee cup shakes in my hand uncontrollably before slipping to the floor. This is what I wanted, right? To be free of him forever? To never hear his voice again. Never feel his fingers digging into my skin. Never see that look of desperate need in his eyes. Falling to my knees, I cry out for him, as my world comes crashing down. A strangled sob gets trapped in my throat, and the world goes black.

Chapter Twenty-One

Bella

The excruciating pain in my head intensifies as I open my eyes, so I shut them quickly. Tears slip down my cheeks as I try to make sense of him being gone, but I can't. My kidnapper. My tormentor. The only man who ever made me feel alive, even though I never would've admitted it to him. I should probably be afraid of his brothers coming after me, but I'm not. Right now, I'd welcome them to come and remove this throbbing from my chest.

Moving to a sitting position, I push the tangled hair out of my face and attempt to take a deep breath, but can't. Even though I told myself he needed to die so I could be free of him, I didn't mean to kill him. What I can't wrap my pounding head around is why I miss him so damn much. My body literally aches for the touch of a man that only wanted to hurt me, and it makes zero sense to me.

"Let the darkness in, living dead girl."

"Nico," I gasp so loud it nearly echoes, but there's no response because he's not here. He's dead.

Getting off the floor, I grab my phone and turn to google for help. I search for, 'can you go crazy after someone dies'. I roll my eyes at my phone, when the search engine informs me that yes, it's common to feel like you're going crazy after a loved one dies.

Loved one?

Nico was hardly a loved one, but it's suddenly becoming clear that I never hated him. I wanted to understand him, but I still don't. His hunger for killing was confusing to me, although if I'm honest with myself, when I killed that man, there was a rush that ran through me. I wasn't willing to acknowledge it, but it was there. He wasn't a good man, and according to Nico, he would've done things worse than him.

I could totally be a serial killer if they were all bad men.

"Let the darkness in, living dead girl."

Why am I hearing his voice? I'm going crazy for sure. Dead people don't talk to you, unless you're insane.

"Let the darkness in, living dead girl."

I scream at him.

"Stop saying that. Just stop. I'm not dark like you."

"Yes, baby, you are."

Jesus, Bella. You're really losing touch with reality here. Stop talking to the dead guy, and his voice will go away.

Yet, he doesn't. He's inside my head and won't stop.

"You want to kill right now, don't you? Do you remember how it felt to squeeze the life out of that asshole? Can you get his glazed over eyes out of your mind, baby? Does his final breath leaving his body stay with you? The power that surged through your body like a live wire is addictive. It's okay to do it again."

Reaching my hands into my hair on either side, I pull so hard that tears spring to my eyes as I scream.

"Go away. I don't need you. Fuck off and leave me alone!"

Once again, I get what I want, and realize it's not what I wanted at all.

"Nico!" I cry.

No response.

I know his voice in my mind was not real, and it was probably a sign of a mental health emergency, but the silence is louder than anything I've ever heard. I attempt to imagine what it felt like to have his arms wrapped around me. The safety and warmth are so far away now, and it leaves me cold.

No, Bella. He was not safety. Nico carved his name in your skin, and did whatever he wanted to you. Remember the spiders?

Even now, I try to hate him to ease the pain, but I can't. I don't know what I truly feel for him, but it's not hatred.

The wind whips through the trees, shaking my windows slightly, and I panic. Once again, I'm on my own. Even though I've lived alone since I moved out of my mom's house when I was seventeen, I still hate it. It's something I've never gotten comfortable with, but I can't turn the television back on, because I can't stomach hearing the words from the newscaster again, telling me once again that Nico is dead.

Typing into google, I search for everything Bonetti, because I know one thing for sure. I'm going to find that graveyard again. I don't know why, but the urge to be there is sudden and strong. There's more information than you'd expect on a mafia family that would likely want to stay under the radar. Apparently, his brother Bones got married not long ago. And his brother Psycho was arrested a year ago, but mysteriously got released, and there was nothing more said about it, which is kind of weird.

Then I find a picture of Nico, and stare at it for what feels like an eternity, as my chest squeezes painfully. He's handsome in a violent way. A strong jaw, no smile, more of a scowl, as he stands talking to another man I don't recognize, but the caption says his name is Damian De Luca. Nico is dressed in his usual black jeans, and a black t-shirt tight enough to show his defined muscles. The tattoos on his forearms show, but of course, his clothing covers the weird eyeball one. I screenshot it and trace my fingers over his jaw.

Sighing audibly, I close out of the photograph and go back to my search, and look for the Bonetti family graveyard, but find nothing.

Closing my eyes, I think back to that night and try to remember every visual clue. The highway that stretched for mile after mile. McDonalds on the right, before he took the exit. But then all I can see in my mind is trees and more trees. Isolation for miles in either direction.

Fuck!

Think, Bella, think.

In a split second decision, I decide to go to the coffee shop, and attempt to retrace his driving from memory. As I get up off the floor and get ready to leave, I hate myself. I'm always too late.

I fall in love with a band a decade after they retire. Get into a book after everybody else is done with it. Movies, same thing. Now this is the worst.

I'm not so fucking lost that I don't realize I shouldn't miss him. I should be relieved he's gone, and I don't have to worry about him doing whatever the hell he wants to me. Relief is not what I feel. Knowing how things should be doesn't change the way they actually are.

I fucking miss him.

Not all aspects. I don't miss the chains or the spiders. That's a hell I'd rather not relive. But him, yeah, I miss it. I wasn't a virgin like he was. I've been with more men that I care to admit. I've had orgasms before. Yet, the way he touched me was different. No man has ever made my body feel that way. That hunger in his eyes was intoxicating. As a woman, it's rare to have someone look at you that way. Nico was intense in all ways. Now that I've screamed his voice out of my head, I want to hear it again. It's a craving that might never go away.

Chapter Twenty-Two

Bella

My first two driving trips looking for the graveyard were a bust. I wanted to give up, but I couldn't. There was something pushing me to find it, even though I don't understand what it is. When I make a wrong turn and notice a familiar scene, I smile to myself from ear to ear.

"Nico, I found it!"

Talking to a dead guy is probably not a good sign. I'm pretty sure I'm going crazy, or maybe I'm already gone, but it's the one thing that helps right now.

Parking my car outside of the black metal fence, I take a deep breath and get out. I walk up to the entrance, but it's locked, so I do what any sane person would do. Placing my foot on the lower bar, I grab the top, and swing my body up and over it. My landing is far less than graceful as I crash onto the ground. Getting up, I dust myself off.

On instinct, I walk over to the grave he tried to kill me on, and drop to my knees, and scream his name.

According to my google search, there are five stages of grief. Denial, anger, bargaining, depression, and acceptance. Denial came and went quickly, because I was there. I saw the knife in his chest. It's pretty difficult to deny that. Anger. That's where I am now, mixed with depression, I suppose. But acceptance? I don't think I'll ever accept what I did to him. I'll never be okay with him being gone.

Why did I have to grab that fucking knife? If I hadn't made that one stupid move, everything would be okay right now.

"Nico. I don't know what to do."

I let the tears fall, as I dig my fingers into the earth beneath me. The very place he planned to take my life and, at this moment, I wish I had let him. I have spent most of my life blocking shit out, not feeling anything, and now it's as if my entire being is nothing but the thing I've avoided most.

I collapse onto the ground, a sobbing mess, when I hear his voice again.

"Let the darkness in, living dead girl."

My brain is fucking with me. Why are those the words my brain is playing on repeat?

After hours of laying on the cold ground, I get up because I need to numb this pain. I have to find a fucking drink.

Walking over to the gate, I try to see if there's a way to get it open, and notice that it unlocks from the inside. I open it and leave it open because I'm coming back. This place has some odd connection to Nico for me. And I know if I come back here, I'll feel him on some level. The emptiness is not as bad as it is in my apartment.

I get in my car and drive back to civilization. The streets are mostly vacant, but my heart stops for a moment, when an ambulance zooms by. It makes me think of the night I stabbed him. I should've stayed, instead of running away like a coward. Is that why he died? Because I called his brother, instead of 9-1-1? Maybe it took Bones too long to get to him. I should have saved him the way I knew he would've saved me.

My vision blurs as I remember that night, as I pull into the parking lot of the only bar I see.

"Bella, I'm an asshole. I know that. But baby, please, you're the only good thing in my life. Please don't do this. I'm begging you. Don't do this to me."

His voice sounded so raw, desperate for me to not end my life. He wasn't pleading for his safety, but mine. And that makes me a bigger monster than he ever was. I wipe my tears away and head into the bar. A dive called *Shots*. Not an especially creative name, but exactly what I'm after. I have no plans on driving drunk, but I do want to numb myself for a little while. I need to.

Walking up to the bar, I order two shots of tequila as I take a seat on a black stool, and the bartender raises an eyebrow.

"Got ID, darlin'?" he drawls, with a southern accent that doesn't quite fit around here.

Opening my purse, I hand him my driver's license and he tips his black cowboy hat.

"Okay, Miss Arabella, top shelf?"

I nod at him. "It's Bella. Top shelf is fine."

He smirks at me as he sets the two shots in front of me with lime and salt.

"Alright, Miss Bella, let me know if you need anything else."

The bar is less dingy than the outside, but it's still not a classy place. It's got a small black bar that's covered in scratches, and six bar stools bolted to the floor. It's a tiny place with only four black tables, and a jukebox with an out-of-order sign taped to it.

Throwing back the first shot, I close my eyes as the burn travels from my throat to my chest. Then, I do the same thing with the second, when a man approaches me and sits on the barstool beside me.

"Hi, beautiful. Can I buy you a drink?"

I shake my head no, as I motion for the bartender to bring me another shot of tequila.

"I'm good. I can buy my own drinks and I'm not interested."

I can feel his glare on me, even though I'm looking straight ahead. I don't need to see it to know it's there.

"No need to be a bitch. What's wrong with you? Take the drink like any other slut and say thank you."

"Let the darkness in, living dead girl."

"Nico," I gasp under my breath, but the asshole beside me hears it.

"Who the fuck is Nico?"

Without bothering to answer this guy, because I don't owe him anything, I toss back my third drink and set money on the bar and leave.

As I walk out to my car, I hear footsteps behind me.

"Get fucking lost, asshole. I said I'm not interested."

Opening my door, I slide into the driver's seat and head back to the graveyard. I know I'm not in a great mood, but that guy was a dick for no reason. If a woman says she isn't interested, just move the fuck on.

I breathe a sigh of relief when I pull back up to the graveyard. The gate is still open, so I walk right through, and take my spot beside my favorite grave. The place where I nearly died, but found something I quickly lost.

A car door slams, and I quickly jump up and see the idiot from the bar coming toward me.

He's wearing dark blue jeans and a wife beater shirt, as well as an angry glare on his face.

"You're a cunt, and a cunt is only good for one thing."

I glare right back at him.

"You fucking followed me here? Asshole."

This stranger stalks toward me.

"Care to tell me why we're in a cemetery?"

I don't respond, and he stops in front of me, and places his hand on my head and pushes down.

"On your fucking knees, whore."

"What? No."

He laughs wickedly.

"You're going to suck my dick, or I'll put a bullet in your brain."

I don't see a gun, but I don't doubt that he has one either.

"Fuck," I mutter under my breath, causing him to laugh louder.

"Let me take my shoes off first."

He stares, from my light pink lacy shirt to my faded jeans, like he's undressing me with his eyes.

98

"Take off whatever you want."

I unstrap my heels and set them beside me on the ground, while he unzips his jeans and pulls them down to his feet. Staring at me, he orders, "Start sucking."

"Let the darkness in, living dead girl."

It's only my imagination, but his voice is comforting, and exactly what I need right now.

Taking his tiny dick in my hand, he groans and closes his eyes. With my free and dominant hand, I pick up my shoe and drive the heel into his balls. He screams as he jumps away from me and falls to the ground.

"I'm going to fucking kill you."

Glancing down at his bleeding skin, I smile at him and climb on top of him, and wrap my hands around his throat.

"Let the darkness in, living dead girl. That's it, baby, squeeze as hard as you can."

Reaching up, he pulls my hair, trying to get me off him, but I hold on for dear life. If it's a choice between him or me, I choose me.

"Stare into his eyes, baby. Watch the light fade."

His eyes widen as he struggles underneath me, and within minutes, he's dead.

"Come here, baby."

Glancing over, I see Nico laying on top of a grave and I walk over to him, knowing he's not real. Laying down with him, I lay my head on his chest and absorb his warmth against my face.

"Nico, I'm sorry."

He strokes his hand through my hair.

"I know, living dead girl. It's okay."

I sob into his chest, and wish I could always feel him like this. He's imaginary and I'm afraid, at any moment, my mind will right itself and he'll be gone forever.

"Sleep, baby. I'm right here."

Chapter Twenty-Three
BELLA

The sun beats down on me through my closed eyelids, giving me an instant headache, as I lay on the cold, hard ground. There's no Nico. That was only my mind, giving me the comfort I desperately needed. I don't believe in ghosts, so I know it wasn't really him, although right now I wish it was.

What was different about last night that made me not only hear him, but see him, and feel him? Was it killing a man? Shit, the man.

I have no idea what to do with him, but at least he's in a graveyard. And I doubt anybody comes out here often. Nico should be buried already. Is he here?

Opening my eyes, I climb to my feet and search for his grave. Is that why I feel him here so strongly? Walking through row after row of graves, I don't find him. Maybe they have more than one cemetery. They certainly have enough money to do that. Most of the graves' death dates are old. The newest is 1950. So maybe this is an old one, and they have a new one somewhere. Some place I'll never find.

"Nico!" I scream, but there's no response, and I know what I have to do. *Kill.* Even from beyond the grave, he's trying to turn me into a serial killer like him. I'll do anything to see him again. Even take another life if I have to.

I sit on the ground with my back toward the dead guy, and with my phone in my hand, and think. Once I have a plan somewhat in place, I say goodbye to Nico.

"I'm sorry. I wish you were here with me. I'll see you tonight, I hope."

After taking a shower, I dress in my favorite black lingerie. A corset and matching panties. The dating site I found, *Sexcapades,* requires a profile photo, and this is probably the best way to reel people in. I know it's wrong. Taking lives is not okay, but I'll do anything to lie in his arms again like I did last night, even if it's only in my mind. I'm not crazy. I've decided that, because I think crazy people don't know shit is only in their head, and I absolutely do. Nico is gone, but I will do whatever I need to hold on to a piece of him. Even an imaginary one.

I snap the picture and post it, with mostly false information.

Name: Michele

Age: 20

Sexual Preference: Bi-Sexual

I cackle at myself because I'm not bi-sexual, but most men have a fantasy of two women together, so that might interest them a little more. It takes less than ten minutes for the messages to start coming in. I respond to Steven first, and ask him to email me off the app, because I want to find out more about him before making my selection. It takes a while, but I finally find the one I want. I'm not like Nico. I don't have an interest in killing for no reason. If I don't find anything on a criminal internet search, I'll move on. Guaranteed, on a site like this, I'll find some bad men, and those are the ones I want the most. I get what I need, and I'm doing the world a favor at the same time. Guilt free killing.

Once I start talking to them about their fantasies, they are like an open book. A guy that thinks he can fuck a woman, and do whatever he wants to her, is rather forthcoming. Finding out their names means I can look up mugshots, as well as arrest information.

Shaking my head, I stare at Michael's most recent mugshot. How did they let this asshole out of prison? Rape of a minor should be a lifetime sentence, or death. I giggle to myself. Sorry, Michael, you're about to be re-sentenced.

After telling him he could do anything he wanted to me, at the location of my choosing, he was like putty in my hands. I have an hour to sew a pocket to hold a knife under my dress, just in case I need it. *Thank you, tenth grade sewing, that I was sure I'd never use.*

I pull on my dress for the evening, a light blue halter dress that falls to the middle of my thigh. It's important I have full use of my arms without restrictions, so even though I may be a little chilly, that's the way to go. Grabbing my phone, I take a moment to look at Nico's picture I screenshotted earlier.

"I miss you, and I'm mad at you. How dare you carve your name into my ass, and then leave me? I know it's my fault, but I'm still angry. I need you, Nico. Look what I've become, all because of you. How many people will I kill, before I can live without your voice? Your touch? Your imaginary eyes on me? Maybe it never ends."

Nico Bonetti changed me. I've always been somewhat damaged, but he solidified it, and I'd rather live in some fantasy world concocted by my brain, than in the real world where he doesn't exist.

Chapter Twenty-Four

Bella

Six Weeks Later...

I glance down at my *Sexcapades* dating app and smile. Blonde hair, blue eyes, and broad shoulders await me tonight. Christian sounds like such a nice name, however, the things he wants to do to me are anything but. I bet his mother thinks he's a good man, he's not. How could I know that? Well, it doesn't take an expert to search online for arrest records. My date tonight stands trial in one year for beating the shit out of his wife. One thing I've learned in the last month of my life is men will agree to nearly anything, if they think they'll get their dick wet.

I still spend most of my time at the graveyard. It's where I feel Nico most, and it has almost become a compulsion.

Coming to the realization that I wanted him, once he was dead, has been the bitterest of pills to swallow. I think I wanted him, but I needed a little control. I wanted a choice, but he gave me none. Being chained up the way I was, took that all away. He stripped me of all dignity, until I convinced myself I hated him. I live with a constant pain in my chest. Sometimes it's sharp and sometimes it's dull, but it never fades completely. My time with Nico changed me, and I'm not the same person anymore. I'm not necessarily proud of it, but this is my way of dealing with it. Getting rid of useless trash. Seven dead bodies, and no one will ever suspect a blonde, standing five foot four at full height, would be capable of such things. I do love being a girl.

I touch up my red lipstick, and adjust the straps on my white dress. It's become a uniform of sorts. Men get excited by the innocent look, but the red lip color says I'm willing to give it all away. Dream on, boys. I lost that a long time ago. Each of these men think they're getting laid. Not a chance. After being with Nico, they wouldn't be able to satisfy me, anyway. I begged him to stop, but now I wish I hadn't. I'm a fucked up mess, because it took him dying for me to gain any clarity.

I walk up to Christian, waiting by the tall gray headstone like an obedient puppy. Giggling inwardly, I can't help myself, I love this. It's like taking candy from a baby. The men on this app live their lives led by their dick.

"Christian," I smile sweetly.

"Fuck. You're even more gorgeous in person."

Lifting my eyelashes slowly, I look up at him, playing the game he wants to play.

"Do you still want to do this?"

He nods slowly while he licks his lips. This is his fantasy. If he were Nico, I'd be into it, but he's not, so there's only one way this little game ends.

"I hope you can catch me."

Taking off, I run into the trees, the same way I did the night Reaper tried to kill me. My heart pounds, in part from the memory, and the physical exertion mixed with the anticipation of what I'm about to do.

I dart to the left, just as he thinks he's about to grab me with a husky, "Gotcha."

Laughing, I stay on the move until I hear him panting like a dog in heat. I may be small, but it's his exhaustion that will give me the upper hand. I've been running since I was ten. Every morning before work, I run a minimum of six miles. It's how I got away from Nico that night, and it's how Christian is going to die. Making a circle, I go back toward the graveyard, because that's where I need him to be, because this is where I feel like Nico is. It's not something I understand, so I've stopped trying.

106

Once I get to what has become my favorite headstone, I fall to the ground crying, with my hand over my face. Like all the ones before him, he rushes over to me, not really concerned about me, more likely to do with whether or not he still gets what he wants. He kneels in front of me and stares at my face.

"Sit back a little. Stop crowding me."

He leans back on his knees and I swing my leg up, kicking him in the face with my heel. Christian falls onto his back and cradles his face, while screaming about what a bitch I am. He's not wrong.

I climb on top of him, straddling his chest.

"Pick your poison. Hands. Knife. Or gun."

I lift my skirt, and he watches me with obvious interest. Pulling the knife from the top of the inside of my dress, I show it to him.

"Try it. Fuck with me."

His eyes are wide with pure panic, and it makes me understand the man known as Reaper a little more.

"What do you want? Money? Take my wallet. Just get the fuck away from me."

I feign a sad expression.

"You don't want to fuck me now?"

He shakes his head emphatically. Apparently, I've killed the mood.

"Lace your fingers behind your head."

Christian hesitates, so I press the tip of my knife into his throat until he complies.

"What's your poison, Christian? This is happening. Take your pick."

He closes his eyes tight.

"Hands."

I smile and sigh contentedly.

"I was hoping you'd say that."

After placing my knife back in the pocket under my skirt, I place my hands around his throat.

"Eyes open."

He blinks his eyes open as a tear trails down his cheek.

"How many times did you make your wife cry?"

Recognition shows on his face, and I know he thinks she sent me. I don't even know her.

"Did she do this?"

I smile softly at him before I reply.

"No. You did this."

Tightening my hands around his throat, I stare into his eyes, as he shakes his head back and forth. He wants to fight me, but he knows his death will be far more bloody and painful. I wait for the moment I hear his words. This is how I know Nico is with me. Every time I kill someone, I hear his voice.

Let the darkness in, living dead girl. Don't fight it. I promise it'll feel good.

As Christian dies, and I don't hear those words, the emptiness fills me once again. Despair. I get off him and fall to my knees beside his dead body.

"Nico," I sob into my hands, and like he was waiting for me to break, his voice is there, in my head once again.

"Living dead girl, this is beautiful, baby, but this trail of dead bodies in my family cemetery is beginning to cause problems."

Turning to the sound, I know I've gone crazy when I lift my gaze, and see him staring at me with a heated expression.

"Nico," I gasp.

Chapter Twenty-Five
REAPER

She looks fucking stunning, broken for me, on her knees, tears on her cheeks, eyes blown wide with her murderous lust, and I have no fucking idea how I've managed to keep my distance from her for six weeks. My neck doesn't tingle with the need to end a life. Instead, my entire body thrums with desire for her, my living dead girl.

I motion for her to come over to me, and she slowly rises to her feet and walks to me, looking like the beautiful angel of death she is. Dressed in white, a picture of innocence, when she is anything but. She reaches me, and immediately places her hands on my chest, as more tears fall.

"Nico."

Sliding my hand into her soft blonde curls, I lean down and inhale her scent. Bella grabs my shirt and speaks low.

"Tell me you're here. Or am I crazy?"

I chuckle softly.

"You're definitely crazy, living dead girl, but I'm here."

Her lashes flutter as she raises her gaze to mine.

"I thought I killed you."

Leaning down, I swipe my tongue over her cheek, tasting her tears, and groan.

"It was fucking close, baby, but I couldn't leave you."

Placing her hand on my face, she stares into my eyes, and my chest squeezes hard. I don't normally live with regrets, but I do now. At this moment, I cannot fathom that I nearly killed this perfect creature. My other half. Yet, had I not, we wouldn't be here right now, with Bella looking at me for the first time with something other than hatred.

I pull her hand from my face, and kiss her knuckles softly, before taking her hand in mine and walking over to where the dead guy is. Letting go of her, I grab his feet and pull him away from the grave.

"What are you doing?" she questions me.

Turning to her, I narrow my gaze at her. "Taking what's mine, where I first wanted to take it, unless you're going to tell me no."

She places her hands on her hips and, fuck, I love that sassy look on her face.

"And you'd listen?"

I smirk at her. "No, baby, but I thought it sounded good."

Running my tongue over my bottom lip, I can already taste her dripping on my tongue.

"Show me my name."

Without any hesitation, she pulls her dress up, removes her white lacy panties, stepping out of them, then she holds her skirt up. I stare at my name. An 'N' and an 'I' on her left cheek, and 'C' and 'O' on her right one.

"Get over here."

She takes a few steps to me and slides her hand under my shirt. I groan from the feeling of her fingertips on my skin. Sliding my hands in her hair, I pull hard, forcing her head back, and run my tongue up the center of her throat. One little whimper escaping from her sweet mouth sends me over the edge. Releasing my grip on her hair, I slide my hands to her face and press my lips to hers. Our kiss muffles her moans, as I slide my tongue against hers. Bella is not an unwilling participant, and right now I'm not sure she ever was.

Pulling back from our kiss so I can look at her, she digs her nails into my skin, as she whimpers my name in a near pant.

Scooping her into my arms, I lay her over the grave and grin, when she spreads her legs so willingly.

"Needy little slut."

Lifting the skirt to her dress up, she flashes me a shy smile as she exposes her bare pussy to me. Do I want to fuck her? Hell yes, I do, but first, I want to see what she does. This new side to her I've never seen before intrigues the fuck out of me.

"Take your shirt off, Nico."

Without a word, I reach back and grab the collar to my t-shirt and pull it off, dropping it on the ground beside me.

The last thing I want to do is talk right now. I need to be inside her, but as I stare at her pussy, my mind won't stop. For the last three weeks, I've been watching her, but before that I was fighting for my life. She thought I was dead, so it wouldn't change things between us, nothing could make me not want her, but I still need to know.

"Did you fuck them, Bella? Any of them?"

My voice comes out strained, as I imagine some dickhead having what's mine.

"No, Nico. I killed them. There was never a chance of me fucking anyone else."

Kneeling between her legs, I ask, "Didn't it get you wet? Having the power to take away human life?"

"Yes," she moans lightly.

"And you didn't fuck anyone?"

She pulls her lip between her teeth and shakes her head.

"I fucked myself."

Jesus Christ, I like that thought a little too much, but it doesn't come as a surprise, since I saw her pleasuring herself right on this very grave.

I undo my pants to release myself, because these jeans are getting too fucking tight.

"Show me, baby."

She drops her gaze to my dick and, with a moan, she pushes a finger inside her, and then two. I watch my living dead girl, laying on a grave and masturbating for me. Not able to take it anymore, I fist my cock as she whimpers for me. Her pussy is drenched, I can hear it, and it's my favorite sound. Second only to her begging for me.

"Nico, please. I need you."

Grabbing her wrist, I pull her fingers out, and bring her hand to my face and inhale her scent. Sucking her wetness, I groan.

"Fuck, I missed this taste, baby. I need more."

Pushing her legs back, I move down and push my tongue inside her and swirl it around. She slides her hands into my hair, but instead of trying to pull me away, she holds me tight against her pussy.

I liked the fight. Her clawing at me, begging me to stop, and when I saw how devastated she was by my death, I wondered if I had her like this, if the thrill would be gone. It's not. I'm as hungry for her as I ever have been. Maybe even more so. Pulling my tongue out of her, I replace it with two fingers and fuck her with them, while I lick at her clit and she writhes around for me. She's a whimpering mess for me. Digging her nails into my scalp, she screams for me in the quiet of the night. Where we are is isolated. There's no traffic to dull the sound of her coming for me. There's only a lone cricket off in the distance, and the way her voice echoes as she begs me to fuck her, is simply too much to bear.

I get back up on my knees and pull my jeans and boxers down, as my girl lays in front of me, looking like a deadly work of art.

Licking her lips, she moans quietly.

Pushing my cock inside her, I grunt because she feels better than the last time I was inside her, and I don't know how that's possible.

"Fuck, baby."

"Nico," she whimpers in response, as I climb over her and place a hand on the grave on either side of her head.

"You're mine, living dead girl. You should know there's a tracker in your ass, and I'll never let you out of my sight. I've been watching you. Six fucking miserable weeks without touching you. Never again."

Pulling out most of the way, I thrust back inside her. Wrapping my hand around her throat, I groan, "Admit the fucking truth, Bella."

Her eyes show that she doesn't know what I'm asking for.

"Tell me you won't run from me. Tell me you're mine."

I pick up my speed, as her pulse beats against my fingers, as I continue fucking her harder.

"Nico!" she screams as her body convulses under mine, but it's her next words that are my absolute undoing.

"I'm yours."

She tangles her hand in my hair and pulls my head back, and stares at me dead in the eyes.

"But you're also mine, and any woman that dreams of touching you is dead."

Her eyes drop to my chest, as unshed tears fill her eyes, and she places her hand on my surgical scar.

"I'm so sorry."

Smirking at her, I speak the truth, "I'm not."

How could I be sorry? There's no doubt in my mind she never would have realized that she felt something for me, if she didn't think I was dead. It's fucked up that it took that much, but it was worth it.

Her eyes register so much pain, and I'm fully aware how much she regrets what happened.

"I could've killed you."

Looking down at her softly, I stroke the side of her face. Guilt will eat you alive if you let it. I don't want that for her.

"Don't, Bella. Let's not live in the past. Stay in the present with me. Focus on my cock driving into your sweet pussy."

Reaching up, she drags her thumb over my bottom lip.

"Kiss me, Nico."

She nearly makes me come right there on the spot. I never thought I'd hear her ask for me to kiss her, and it causes my head to spin. Gripping her chin, I lower my head and taste her lips again. First it's soft and slow, but it becomes urgent as I hammer her pussy. Every little whimper that escapes from her causes me to fuck her harder, as I chase my release.

Chapter Twenty-Six

BELLA

He comes with a grunt so sexy I wish I could record it, and hear it over and over again. Rolling over onto his back, he pulls me into his arms.

"What have you been up to for the last month and a half, living dead girl?"

I roll my eyes at him, because I'm pretty sure he doesn't just know about some, he knows about them all.

"How long have you been watching me?"

Running his hand up the outside of my thigh, he admits, "Since the day I got out of the hospital. Three weeks. I watched you kill five men. I was ready to intervene if they got the upper-hand, but they never did. You moved gracefully, with the confidence of a skilled assassin, yet still appeared dainty. I don't think I've ever seen anything more beautiful."

I slide my hand along the weird eyeball tattoo on his shoulder as he stares at me.

"Why didn't you show yourself to me, Nico? I felt like I was dying."

He kisses me on the forehead.

"Honestly, you needed more time. And I wanted to see how long it would go on for."

Narrowing his gaze at me, he growls, "I will be deleting that app from your phone. You're lucky I stayed away long enough to get over you showing yourself in lingerie on that site. I nearly lost my mind, until I saw that you were only killing them."

I giggle softly.

"Only? Nico, there's something wrong with us."

With a groan, he tugs my bottom lip with his teeth.

"I need to get you home so I can fuck you again, but there's the matter of your dead guy. If my brother finds another dead body here, I'm going to hear more bitching than I can possibly tolerate."

We both get up, and I grab my panties and slide them on under my dress, while he tucks himself into his pants, and I smile when he shoves his t-shirt into his back pocket, instead of putting it back on. Nico with a bare chest is a feast for the eyes.

He catches me staring at him and asks, "What?"

My face heats as I admit, for the first time, that he's attractive.

"I was thinking that I'm glad you didn't cut my eyes out, because not seeing your gorgeous body would be a tragedy."

He feigns shock.

"That's all you want me for? My body? I feel so used."

Chuckling, he walks over to me and takes my hand in his.

"Come on, we need shovels to bury this asshole. By the way, baby, you can use my body anytime you want to."

"Shovels?" I ask as he takes me toward a gray building, and he chuckles.

"That's right, living dead girl. Like myself, you're going to have to dispose of your own bodies. If we went fishing, I'd expect you to not be a girl about it, and put the worm on the hook. If you kill someone on your own, you'll finish the job, which is getting rid of the body. Lucky for you, I've done most of the work for you, so it'll be easy."

We walk into the building that looks like an expensive shed. He grabs two shovels from a hanging rack and hands me one.

"Don't the mafia have people that do this? For their job?"

We walk back outside, and I follow him around to the other side of the building.

"Yes, baby, but remember, I don't work for my family, so I'm on my own. Honestly, before you, I never knew what to do with the bodies, and it caused problems. When you began dropping men like flies, I realized what better place than a graveyard."

He nods to the dirt in front of me.

"Start digging up the loose dirt and don't fall in, please don't fucking fall in. I'm going to go get your friend."

I roll my eyes and do as he told me to. It doesn't take long to see that he has already dug this grave, and the dirt was simply covering up a sheet of plywood over the grave. I set the shovel on the ground and wait.

Nico comes back, carrying Christian over his shoulder, and complains, "This fucker is heavier than he looks."

I remove the plywood as Nico approaches me, and drops him into the hole, and I jump back from the loud thud.

"How deep is that?"

With a grin, he says, "Six feet, baby. There's another six ready to go, and depending on the size of the body, I can fit at least four in each. I wasn't sure when you would take some time off from your new hobby."

Crossing my arms over my chest, I glare at him.

"Are you judging me, Nico Bonetti?"

He shakes his head no.

"Not a chance, living dead girl. I fucking love it. And," he pauses with a groan, "I can't wait to see it again."

He takes my hand and walks me to my car.

"Give me your phone."

Opening my car, I fish it out of my purse and hand it to him.

"What are you doing?"

Staring at me with amusement, he grins at me.

"Two things. Deleting your account from that fucking app. And typing my address into your GPS. I'll be following you. There's a good chance I'll never take my eyes off you again."

Rolling my eyes at him, I say, "That's not realistic, Nico. I have to go home in the morning, so I can get ready for work."

"No," he says with a stern expression.

"Nico, be reasonable. I have bills to pay."

He shakes his head. "No. The answer is fucking no, Bella. You're mine, and that means you're with me, not at some fucking coffee shop, serving assholes that don't deserve your time. You will not have bills. Everything you need will be yours."

"Nico, no."

Stepping forward, he pushes me until my back hits the closed door of my car, and slides his hand from my abdomen all the way to my throat, and stares at me with a pained expression.

"I will give you anything you want, baby, but not this. Being away from you was excruciating, and I won't live through that again. This is non-negotiable. Understood?"

Nodding slowly, I say, "On one condition. Well, two."

He stares into my eyes, waiting for me to elaborate, so I do.

"No chains and no spiders, Nico. I can't live like that."

Sliding his hand from my throat to my face, he cups my cheek, and I nearly crumble from his tenderness.

"No chains and no spiders."

I swing my arms around his neck and pull him down to me. Pressing my face into his neck, I inhale his scent and kiss his skin softly.

"Thank you."

He groans into my hair.

"We need to go because you're driving me fucking crazy. I'm thirty seconds away from fucking you on top of your car."

I giggle and bite his neck.

"Let's go home, and you can fuck me however you want to."

When Nico smiles at me, it's sexy, dangerous, and for some reason, feels like it's only for me and makes my heart pound.

"I want to kiss you, but I'm not going to because we'll never leave if I do, so be a good girl and get in your fucking car. I'll be right behind you."

He hands me my phone, and steps away from me and walks over to his black Range Rover, and I get into my car with a heavy sigh.

Nico is alive.

Life doesn't always give second chances, and I'm not wasting this one.

Chapter Twenty-Seven
REAPER

We should've left her piece of shit car there and she would be sitting beside me. Having her in front of me, but too far away to touch, is fucking torture. I spent as much time away from her as I can tolerate. When I saw her tonight, I knew it was time. After I got out of the hospital, I had every intention of finding her and taking her again. She is mine, after all, but when I saw what she was doing, it changed things. I had to let her discover that we aren't that different. She thought I was a homicidal maniac, and she wasn't wrong, but now she knows she is too. We were cut from the same cloth, and now I have my missing piece.

Bones wanted to kill her, after he found out it was her hand on the knife that nearly took my life. There was no chance I'd ever allow that to happen. He finally agreed, but ordered me to stay away from her. That also wasn't an option. Even if I knew she'd kill me, I'd risk it, just to touch her once more. I'll always crave one more look, one more touch, one more kiss. There will never be a day where I don't need more of her than I've already had. My brothers all think I'm insane, but they've thought that for nearly my entire life. We all like hurting people, but I'm the only one that searches for people to kill for no reason other than the rush. Kage was the first I told about the tingling in my neck. His response was, 'that's not fucking normal'.

Fuck normal. I live my life unapologetically, and now I have someone that gets me. We still have a lot to learn about each other, but for now, I know enough.

Finally, she pulls onto my property and, using my phone, I open the gates. I have security, but it's not like my brothers' homes, because I don't work with the mafia. However, even if I didn't kill people for fun, I'd still be at risk, simply because I'm a Bonetti, so I have four guards around the clock. To most people, they'd think that is a lot, but it pales in comparison to Bones and Athena's house. Now that Bella will be with me, I may need to rethink my security situation. She will automatically become a target because of me, and I'll never allow anything to happen to her. She parks near the fountain and I pull in behind her, and quickly get out of my Range Rover to get to my girl. The familiar tingling in my neck is replaced with fingers itching to touch her.

I walk purposefully to her, with a fire in my veins, and slide my hand into her hair, pulling her head back. I groan before slamming my lips to hers. She whimpers into my mouth, as she wraps her arms around my neck and digs her nails into my skin.

Fuck.

Bella tastes like heaven and hell mixed together. Good and bad. A prayer and sin. She's everything wrapped up in an alluring package. Her tongue tangles with mine in a fight of dominance. I slide my hand from her hair, and place it around her throat, to remind her who's in charge. Her response is intoxicating. She places her hand over mine and squeezes, as a whimper escapes from her throat.

Pulling back from her, I narrow my gaze at her, my heart pounding in my chest at what this woman does to me.

"Go bend over the fountain."

She immediately does as she's told, as I pull my phone out and disable the cameras over here. I do not want the guys in the guard shack watching this. I'd have to kill them, and I wouldn't mind, except then I'd have to find new ones to replace them.

Grabbing my knife from my back pocket, I slice down the back of her dress, and she glares at me from over her shoulder.

"This was one of my favorites."

I smirk at her.

"I'll buy you twenty more."

Kneeling behind her, I pull her panties down to her feet, and am in awe of her beautiful ass. My name, like a neon sign, telling me everything I need to know. Tracing my fingers over the letters I carved in her skin, I ask her, "Do you know why I did this?"

"Because you're an asshole who likes to hurt me?"

I chuckle, while digging my fingers into the 'n' and the 'o'.

"I am an asshole, and yes, I like to hurt you, but that's not why, baby. I did this because I wanted you to always know who owns you. I'll never kill you, because I can't fucking live without you. Instead, I'll keep you forever. My perfect little pet."

Glaring at me from over her shoulder, she bites, "And who owns you, Reaper?"

I grin at her.

"Reaper?"

Through clenched teeth, she says, "When I'm mad at you, from now on, it's Reaper."

I run my tongue over my bottom lip. Fuck, I like her like this. Angry Bella is sexy as fuck.

Drawing my hand back, I smack her naked ass hard, causing her to yelp.

"It's fucking Nico. Don't let me hear you call me anything else, unless you prefer Master. To answer your question, *you* own me, living dead girl. You have since the first fucking moment I saw you. Now that I have seen what you're capable of, everything is clear as day. You're mine and I'm yours."

"Then I should carve my name into your skin," she growls, in a pretty fucking voice that makes my cock throb, and shreds my control.

"Any fucking time, baby."

I pull my pants down and line my cock up with her beautiful pussy, and push inside her with a groan. Grabbing her hips, I pull out of her most of the way, before jack-hammering her. Her hands grip on the metal fence surrounding the fountain, and water splashes on her as I fuck her while she moans for me. All her anger is gone as she cries for me.

"Nico!"

"Good fucking girl. Give me everything."

"Goddamn it, Nico," she complains, and I'm thoroughly confused.

"What, baby?"

"Fucking choke me," she screams at me.

She doesn't have to tell me twice. I slide my hand up her back to her neck, and then around her throat.

"Perfect fucking slut," I say as I squeeze slightly, while I move in and out of her drenched pussy. Her whimpers vibrate against my palm, as her cunt clenches down on my cock like it never wants to let me go.

"Good girl," I growl as she trembles beneath me, giving me the one thing I crave most.

Her orgasm.

Even when she was fighting this thing between us, she always came, and I somehow got addicted to it. Like any other man, I enjoy my own orgasms, but hers are what drive me insane. Watching her unravel for me, even if she doesn't want to, is a high no other drug could compete with. We all have our own things we get off from. For some people, it's alcohol or drugs. Most of my life that high came from killing people, but now it's her. I'm not going soft. I'll still end lives, but she'll be with me, and after we're done, I'll fuck her relentlessly while I restrict her breathing. If I could have scripted my own life, it would've never been this good.

I squeeze her throat a little tighter, and she whimpers helplessly as I pound her into another orgasm. Releasing her throat, she gasps as I grip onto her ass on either side, and grunt as I finish inside her.

Chapter Twenty–Eight

BELLA

I gaze at him with a questioning expression as he pulls my panties back up, and he chuckles in response.

"I'm a gentleman, living dead girl."

Rolling my eyes at him, I say, "I think that's up for debate."

He hoists me over his shoulder and carries me inside the house.

"I can walk, you know."

Speaking flatly, he says, "I have security, and I don't want to risk them seeing your exposed body."

I consider telling him that, had he not shredded my dress, he wouldn't have to worry about it, but I let it go, because I already have things to tell him that might change everything between us. The moment I learned he was still alive, I knew things wouldn't be what he thinks they are.

He climbs the stairs and takes me to the bedroom, and sets me down, and all the air escapes from my lungs. I stare at the spot where I left him, *dying*.

"Baby, what is it?"

I shake my head. "Nothing."

Dragging his fingers down my cheek, he speaks low, and I can hear the anguish.

"You're staring at the spot I sat in, with a knife in my chest, and you have tears rolling down your cheeks. Don't tell me it's nothing when it's clearly something."

He cradles my chin and lifts my gaze to his, and I touch my face that I didn't even know was wet. I was so lost in what happened here before, I didn't even realize I was crying.

"You should kill me, Nico. Isn't that what your family does when someone hurts them? Or tries to kill them?"

He chuckles softly.

"Yeah, baby, it is, but there's a couple of problems with that. One, I can't fucking live without you. And two, you weren't trying to kill me. Instead, you were trying to destroy my entire world. For that you can be sorry, but everything that happened after was not your responsibility."

Walking over to the dresser, he grabs a t-shirt and hands it to me.

"We'll get your clothes tomorrow, but this will have to do for now."

I shimmy out of the dress that's barely hanging on my body, and pull the shirt over my head.

"Thank you."

He does his pants back up and plops down on the bed, and opens his arms with a serious expression.

"Come here, baby. Let me give you what you need."

More tears fall, because somehow he does know I need him to hold me. I need a few more minutes in his arms, before I shatter the world we're so content in. I kick my shoes off, climb into his embrace, and he holds me tight against his chest. Laying my head against his beating chest, the guilt nearly consumes me. I know I probably should simply be happy he's alive, and I am, but I can't get over how close he came to death because of my choices.

"What made you decide to kill?"

I sigh audibly.

"The first attacked me. After following me from a bar to the graveyard, he told me to either suck his dick, or he was going to kill me. When I killed him, I heard your voice. My mind gave me the gift of you, but only when I took lives. I could hear you, smell you, feel you, and sometimes even see you and touch you. It was the only way I could have you."

Anybody else would judge me, and call me a crazy bitch, but not Nico. He just kisses me on the head and says, "I missed you too,

126

baby. God. I fucking missed you so much. I thought I would die all over again."

I pop my head up and stare at him.

"All over again?"

He nods slowly.

"Yeah, I died on the way to the hospital. I had to be revived."

"Nico," I gasp as the pain fills me completely.

"Enough, Bella. Let it go. It happened. I'm alive. Having you like this makes it all worth it."

Placing his hand on my face, he stares into my eyes while he admits, "I never thought I was capable of anything other than hate. I'm mostly evil, but for you, I have love. Something I never thought was possible. When I saw you, believing I was dead, and you were so broken, I knew the truth, baby. Maybe you won't admit it, but you love me too."

Love? That's not something I've even thought about, but how else do you describe being so desperate for someone that you're willing to take lives, just to hear the person's voice again? I don't think there's any other reasonable explanation.

"I love you too, Nico."

He tilts his head and asks, "Why are you blushing? Are you embarrassed to admit that you love me?"

I shrug my shoulders.

"I don't know. It's weird. Those aren't words I've said to anyone before. I wasn't a virgin before, but you're my first in this way, and I never thought I loved you, but it makes sense. My life hasn't been easy. I've been through many points of heartbreak, but when I saw, on the news, you were dead..."

I close my eyes and shake my head. When I reopen them, he's still staring at me.

"I've never felt devastation so great. The emotional pain so excruciating, it radiated through my entire body. I didn't honestly know why I felt like that, but now it makes sense. I love you. Even though I've never known what love was."

Wrapping his arms around my waist, he flips me over to my back. Hovering over me, he stares at me with a heated expression.

"What are you doing?"

He pulls himself out of his pants, reaches under his t-shirt I'm wearing, and pushes my panties to the side.

"I need to be inside you, living dead girl."

"Are you ever not hard?" I ask, as he slides inside me.

He smirks at me before shaking his head.

"With you around? No, baby. If I could stay inside this pussy twenty-four hours a day, I would. Now be a good girl and tell me those words again."

Hovering over me, with one hand on the mattress, he cradles the side of my face with the other, while I give him what he wants.

"I love you, Nico."

His hand trembles slightly, as he moves in and out of my pussy, and the features on his face, for once, show emotion.

"I'll still hurt you, because I need it. Your tears are beautiful, so I'll still make you cry, but I'll protect you with my fucking life."

Leaning his head forward, he places his lips on mine, and kisses me like I'm everything he has ever needed. No one has ever made me feel more complete, but there's a danger in feeling so content. Like a house of cards, it could tumble easily.

"Tell me this never ends, Nico. Swear to me, I'm not going to lose you."

Chapter Twenty-Nine
REAPER

Wrapping my hand around her throat, I growl as I come inside her.

"Never."

She responds with an orgasm of her own, and trembles under me, her heart pounding into my chest, as she arches her back and shoves her tits against me. This is how I want us. Connected, as physically close as two people can be, her skin pressing against mine, as she calls my name. There is nothing as beautiful as this, but her questioning if this will last bothers me.

Pulling out of her, the frustration grows until my neck tingles.

"I want you downstairs in ten minutes. We need to talk. And if I stay in this room with you, I'm going to fuck you over and over again."

She pulls the t-shirt down over her legs, and stares at me with concern.

"Did I do something wrong? You look angry."

I run a hand through my hair and shake my head.

"Just hurry up," I say, as I zip my jeans back up.

She isn't just the first woman I've fucked, Bella is my first everything. I've never had a relationship with a woman, and I don't know what's fucking normal and what's not, but I didn't like her questioning whether or not this was fleeting. If she tries to leave me down the line, I am afraid of what I might do to her, because existing without her isn't an option.

I go into the kitchen and look in the refrigerator to make something for her to eat. The tingling in my neck grows, as my frustration mounts.

"Control it," I growl at myself.

Killing is how I've always handled anger, and I can't do that now. Not with her. Not ever.

Taking a deep breath, I get cheese from the refrigerator and take it to the counter, grabbing a knife and cutting board.

"There you are," she says.

I turn to her, and she instinctively steps back as I stare at her, gripping the knife in my hand.

"Nico," she says, almost like it's a warning, and she steps further back until she's standing in the entryway.

Shaking my head, I say, "I don't stab people."

"Your eyes, Nico. They're so dark. I can feel your hostility. You want to kill me. Right now, you're thinking about it."

I nod. "The urge is there, but I can control it."

She steps back further until she's out of view, and like a punch to the gut, all the air in my lungs disappears, leaving me with the same panicked feeling I had when she had the knife to her throat.

Setting what she perceives as a weapon on the cutting board, I walk calmly to the living room, and find her glancing between the kitchen and the door. The panic intensifies, as I realize she's considering running from me.

"Baby, come here. Now."

Staring into my eyes, a tear rolls down her cheek as she walks over to me timidly, everything she's not. I wrap my arms around her and pull her tight against me, as I inhale the calming scent of her hair. I'm more fucked up than I realized.

"Fuck. I'm sorry. I only know one way to handle anger and frustration."

Placing her arms around my back, she presses her face into my bare chest, and says, "That's the first time I've been truly afraid of you, Nico. I can't live like that. You have to find a new way of dealing with things. I'll cut the fucking tracker out of my ass myself, and you'll never see me again."

130

If she were any other woman, I wouldn't believe her. My living dead girl would do something crazy like that without batting an eye. And she's right, constant fear that I'll kill her isn't something that should be part of the equation.

"I'll do better. I don't know how, but I will."

Tilting her head back, her lashes flutter as she raises her gaze to mine.

"I'm not the enemy, Nico. There will be times I make you mad, or upset you, but I'm always on your side."

Reaching up, she presses her hand to my face, while I lean down and press my forehead to hers.

"This is not temporary. It's permanent. Bella, if you leave me, I'll search for you, and either find you or die trying. That's not a threat, it's a promise. You've become my sole reason for breathing. If you go, please plunge the fucking knife into my chest again before you do, because I refuse to exist without you."

Sliding her hand from my face, her fingers travel down my chest, causing an entirely different type of tingling, as she whispers, "What now?"

I smirk at her.

"Now, you're going to eat. I was making you grilled cheese, because it's either that or cereal, because I haven't done any shopping."

She tosses her head back and laughs.

"Grilled cheese happens to be my favorite."

Taking her hand, I pull her back to the kitchen.

"Have a seat on the island."

I go back to slicing the cheese, and preheating the frying pan, while she watches me.

"How old are you?" She asks quietly.

"Twenty-six."

As I'm cooking our food, she continues asking me questions.

"Who was the man at the graveyard that first night?"

I turn to her with a grin. "My brother, Bones."

Her face shows a knowing expression, as her mouth forms a perfect 'O'.

"I expected him to find me and kill me, after what I did."

"He wanted to," I say, as I place the sandwiches on two plates, turn the stove off, and bring the food to the island.

"And now?"

Taking a seat across from her, I tell her what she wants to know.

"He knows you're not to be touched."

I point to the sandwiches.

"Eat."

She picks up her sandwich and takes a bite, and I do the same. I fucking love seeing her like this. It's more than I expected. I knew seeing her naked, with my cock inside her, would be perfect, but watching her eat in my house like this, not chained up, it's far more exciting than it probably should be. I've never had fantasies about sharing my life with a woman, but with her, I want to give her the entire world.

"What?" she asks with pink cheeks, after realizing I'm staring at her.

"I like this normalcy. Having you here with me."

She arches an eyebrow at me.

"Careful, people will think Reaper Bonetti has gone soft."

I chuckle loudly.

"Let's get you some clothes, and then I'll take you for a stroll, to prove that I am not."

Chapter Thirty

Bella

"Do you ever think you'll stop?"

He gets up and grabs two wine glasses, and pours us both a glass of white wine, which might be a strange pairing with grilled cheese, although I'm no expert.

Setting the bottle down, he returns to his seat.

With a goofy grin, he says, "That depends on what you're referring to, baby. Fucking you? That's definitely a no. Looking hot as hell? Also a no."

I roll my eyes at him.

"Always so cocky. I was referring to you killing people. Do you think you'll ever stop?"

He chuckles. "No. It's who I am, although if my brother has his way, I'll reign it in and only kill under specific circumstances."

I raise an eyebrow, and he says, "Enemies. Bad guys. That sort of thing."

I take a sip of my wine, and it's actually not bad with the grilled cheese.

"Are you going to do that?"

He shrugs. "I don't know if I can. The urges are really hard to control. You're the only person I've been able to control it with."

"How often do you do it?"

Taking a sip of his wine, he swallows it, and sets his glass down on the glass table.

"Sometimes it's several times in a week, and then others there might be months between. I don't do it daily, just when I have to. Please, Bella, don't ask me to stop."

I shake my head. "I won't. This is who you are and I accept you as you are, Nico. I don't know if I'll do it again. They weren't innocent men and, honestly, I did it so I could have you with me again."

"You will do it again," he says, and adds to his statement, when I glare at him.

"Not because I'll force you to, because I won't. You will, because I believe you have the same darkness inside you, and I think you'll have the urge to do it. Can you deny it's a rush?"

The way he stares at me, it's like he knows everything. Like I don't have to say a word, and he can read me that well.

"How much did you see in the graveyard, when you were watching me?"

In those moments, I wanted to hear him, but thought I was alone with *the Nico* my imagination dreamed up.

His knowing smile is telling. He saw far more than I knew.

"Yes, baby, I saw you. I watched while you laid there on top of the grave, your hand inside your panties, making yourself come while you screamed my name."

I place my face in my hands, as my cheeks burn with mortification.

"Nothing to be embarrassed about. I've never seen anything more beautiful in my life. It was so difficult not to show myself and touch you. I took my cock out right there, as I stared at you through the bars on the gate, and came with you, baby. And one day soon you'll do it for me again, because I like watching you like that. My pretty living dead girl making herself fall apart for me. Fucking stunning."

He types away on his phone, and then sets it on the table.

Narrowing his gaze at me, he says, "Go take a shower. My brother will be here shortly to bring you clothing, and I don't want him seeing you like this."

"Stay upstairs then?"

Running his tongue over his bottom lip, he stares at me hungrily.

"The t-shirt is fine, baby. I don't want him seeing you freshly fucked, with cum running down your legs."

134

"Oh my God, Nico."

I look at him through spread fingers covering my face, and he motions for me to come to him. Shaking my head, I get up and go over to him, as he scoots his chair out and lifts me onto his lap. He grabs onto the back of my hair and pulls my head back, and runs his tongue up the center of my throat, making me whimper softly.

Moving his hands to my ass, he holds onto me as he rises from the chair, and starts walking. I wrap my arms around his neck so I don't fall, and ask him, "Where are we going? I thought I was taking a shower, and you were waiting for your brother?"

He says matter-of-factly, "That was the plan, but I need you, so I'll take a shower with you."

"You're going to break my pussy, Nico."

Chuckling, he says, "You're a good girl, you can take it."

I scowl at him, feigning irritation.

"Reaper, *the pussy killer,* Bonetti, you better take it easy this time."

He laughs hard as he sets me down in the bathroom, and takes my face in his hands.

"Hot and funny, that's a good combination, living dead girl."

Kissing me softly, he steps away from me and turns the shower on, while I remove the shirt I'm wearing. Turning to me, he stares at me while he gets out of his jeans and boxers. My eyes drop to his already hard cock, and sore or not, I want him inside me again. I get into the shower, and he gets in beside me, before closing the glass door. It's spacious, big enough for at least four people, with stainless steel taps. The walls are painted a masculine dark green. Moving closer to me, he brushes his thumbs over my nipples.

"If you don't like anything, we'll redecorate. My home is now yours, and I want you to be happy here."

Leaning down, he swirls his tongue around my nipple before biting it, making me gasp.

"Nico," I moan as he gives the other one the same treatment, before dropping to his knees. His gaze travels up and down my body, and I shiver from his perusal.

"Fucking gorgeous, baby. A feast for the tongue and the eyes."

He taps the inside of my thigh and I spread my feet further apart, and like he's been dying for it, Nico presses his face against my pussy with a groan, and sucks my clit into his mouth. I reach down and place my hands on his head for stability, as his tongue lashes at me wildly.

Pushing two fingers inside me, he fucks me while I come undone, screaming for him, begging for more.

Taking his fingers out of me, he rises to his full height with a smirk on his face.

"This pretty pussy doesn't appear to be broken to me."

"Not yet, it's not," I say, giggling.

He takes my hands and puts them on his shoulders and warns me.

"Hold on. I'm going to fuck you hard and fast, because my brother is likely downstairs waiting for us. We probably have about ten minutes before he storms in here."

I narrow my gaze at him.

"We can wait then. It's not like we haven't had sex today, Nico."

Ignoring my comment, he grabs the backs of my thighs and lifts them over his forearms, and pushes his cock inside me. Lifting me up, he slams me back down repeatedly.

Holding onto him with my arm around his neck, I touch his face with the other, and place my lips to his. The sensation is intense between our kiss and him fucking me, and I'm moments from unraveling, whimpering loudly, when I hear a voice.

"Hey, asshole, you asked me to bring this shit."

I pull back from our kiss as my heart slams into my chest.

"Get the fuck out, dick!" Nico screams at the man I assume is his brother.

He chuckles obnoxiously. "Hurry the fuck up, before I show you how it's done."

Setting me down, he says, "We'll finish this later. After I fucking kill Kage."

Stepping out of the shower, he turns to me and orders me, "Get washed up, but don't leave the bathroom, until I bring clothes to you. I mean it, Bella."

I hold my hands up.

"Got it, Nico. It's not like I want your brother to see me naked."

Under his breath, he says, "No, but you probably will once you see him."

Grabbing the soap, I clean my body instead of responding, because I don't think I was supposed to hear him.

Chapter Thirty-One
REAPER

I storm out of the bathroom and slam the door, while my asshole brother sits on my fucking bed. Opening a drawer, I pull out a pair of jeans and put them on, and walk over to Kage. I pull my fist back and hit him in the jaw. He jumps up, touching his face, and glares at me.

"What the fuck is wrong with you, Reaper?"

Wrapping my hand around his throat, I growl, "You don't fucking touch her. Don't look at her. You sure as fuck don't come into my bathroom while I'm fucking her. This one is off limits to you, Kage."

He stares at me like I have two heads, as I release my loose grip on his throat.

"You're lucky I don't lay you out, asshole."

I don't say anything back, instead I grab the clothes and bring them to Bella, in the bathroom.

"Get dressed, baby."

She doesn't say anything, but watches me with a concerned expression. I close the door behind me and walk back into the bedroom.

"What the fuck is going on with you?" Kage asks, still rubbing his jaw.

Crossing my arms over my chest, I stare at him. He is not enough of an idiot that he doesn't know why I'm pissed off.

"She's mine. Do you think if you walked in on Bones fucking Athena, that he wouldn't punch you in the fucking face?"

He holds his hands up in defeat.

"Alright, I was just messing around. Maybe I took it too fucking far, but she's just some pussy. Athena is his wife. There's a difference."

Unfolding my arms, I step closer to him. "She is not 'some pussy'. Alright? Bella is mine. Not for today or tomorrow. Fucking forever."

His lips lift up into a grin I'd like to wipe off his face.

"You went and fell in love with the first woman you fucked, didn't you?"

The bathroom door opens, and she comes out, looking gorgeous as always. Kage stares at her with an amused expression.

"Oh, now I get it. Good job, little brother."

Kage is an asshole, but I'm probably closest to him out of my brothers, although I'm more like Psycho.

"Watch it," I say as Bella comes over and stands beside me.

"Bella, this is Kage. Kage, this is my girl, Bella."

He nods at her.

"I'd shake your hand, but I'm afraid Killer here would bite it off."

"Thank you for the clothes," she says sweetly.

"Yeah, thanks, but you can go now, dickhead."

With a grin, he turns to the door and Bella grabs my hand. "Nico," she warns.

I sigh as Kage turns to me with an even bigger smile.

"Nico?"

He chuckles and says, "Alright, I'm leaving before I get hit again."

"That was intense," she says after he leaves.

I pull her into my arms and hold her tight against my chest, and inhale the scent of her freshly washed hair.

"That shouldn't have happened."

Kissing her on the top of the head, I move away from her reluctantly.

"Let me finish getting dressed and we can go."

Grabbing a shirt, I get dressed while Bella keeps asking questions.

"Why did you hit him?"

I pull my boxers on and answer her.

"Several reasons. He never should've come into my bedroom knowing you are here. Kage sure as fuck shouldn't have come into the bathroom where I was fucking you. And finally, his comment about fucking you was out of line. He's lucky I only hit him once."

As I get into my jeans, she continues our conversation.

"Well, it takes two people to fuck, Nico, and I would never. I didn't fuck anyone when I thought you were dead, and I sure as hell wouldn't now. Especially not your brother. You have nothing to be jealous of. I'm with you."

I pull my shirt over my head.

"Kage is a playboy, like Bones used to be. He fucks more women than I can count, and seems to have them lined up. They see him, and immediately fall to their knees for him. And you're exactly his type. I knew if he saw you, he'd think you were beautiful."

She saunters over to me, looking sexy as hell, and strokes her fingers down my cheek.

"Vulnerable Nico is very sexy, but you have nothing to worry about, because I'm yours."

With a grin, she says, "My ass even says so."

I chuckle and kiss her quickly.

"Let's go. I'm going to show you my second favorite thing to do."

I take her hand, and we walk downstairs when she asks, "What's your favorite, if this is second?"

Chuckling, I say, "Fucking you, living dead girl. That's hands-down my favorite thing to do."

Pulling her bottom lip between her teeth, she gazes at me, as I open the door to take her out for the night.

Chapter Thirty-Two
BELLA

"Are they usually women?"

He glances at me from the driver's seat, as he cruises down the road to I don't know where. Nico didn't say where we were going, or how he selects his victims.

"Not necessarily. Some of them have been women, but gender doesn't matter."

I look out the window at the cars driving beside us on the highway. It's not heavy traffic, but we aren't alone either.

"How do you decide?"

His mouth turns up into a wide grin as he chuckles softly.

"I think you already know the answer to that question, baby. It's the eyes. Either they fascinate me, and I want to watch them die, or I don't."

I nod my understanding.

"Like with me."

He agrees, "Like with you. I wasn't looking for someone, but then you were standing in front of me. You lifted your head, looked me in the eyes, and fuck, I was mesmerized."

I giggle as I watch the road in front of us.

"Were you angry when I ran away?"

Reaching down, he grips my thigh, digging his fingers into my bare skin.

"No. I was hard as a fucking rock. Generally, fear paralyzes people and they can't run, but you, fuck, that was hot. The way you took off when we thought you were dead. Silent as you made it through the leaves that should've crunched, and given you away. It fucking enthralled me. I knew I had to have you."

He watches me as I undo my seatbelt, and questions me.

"What are you doing?"

Reaching over, I unbutton and unzip his jeans, with a slight smile on my face.

"Taking what I want."

Sliding my hand into his boxers, I grip his cock in my hand and he groans.

"Fuck."

I undo my seatbelt and move to my knees on the seat and take him out of his underwear, running my tongue up and down his length, before swirling it over the head, causing him to hiss through a clenched jaw.

I take him into my mouth, and suddenly the car stops moving.

"I pulled over so I can watch you."

Placing his hands in my hair, he pulls it away from my face, as I move up and down on his cock. While I can't see his face, I can feel his eyes on me, and it's a powerful moment for me. Giving him what I never give a man. Not willingly.

"You're so fucking beautiful. Jesus fuck, baby, just like that," he groans as I deepthroat him.

Tears leak from my eyes as his cock hits the back of my throat, and I whimper around him.

Holding my head down, he lifts his hips and fucks my mouth, as he grunts his release.

"Fucking drink it, all of it."

Of course, I do and lift my head when he releases me, and I stare at him while licking the small amount of cum that leaked onto my lips.

"Jesus, baby. You're fucking everything."

I sit back in my seat and re-fasten my seatbelt, as he tucks himself back into his pants and zips them up.

Nico grabs my hand and pulls it to his face, kissing my knuckles softly. He doesn't let go as he pulls back out into traffic, and I might never want him to. The more time I spend with him like this, the more I fall. I'm sure any half qualified therapist would say I'm as nuts as he is, since I'm not trying to talk him out of killing someone tonight. I don't want to though. I'm far more excited than I should be, to see him in a murderous rage. Will he be calm or will he be erratic? I can't help but wonder if one person will be enough, or will Nico need more? What if we go on a murderous spree and can't stop? How far can bloodlust go? The notion that I don't want to do this, and only did it to be with Nico again, is long gone. The anticipation of watching him end a life makes it all clear. He's right, I do want this, and I will do it again.

"Are you nervous? You look antsy."

I shake my head. "Excited, not nervous."

He chuckles softly as he turns into a parking lot.

"See. My fucking beautiful, living dead girl. I see you. And you're fucking perfection."

The words 'I see you' slam into my chest, because I've spent most of my life not being seen. The weird girl that doesn't have friends, only acquaintances. Her own mother doesn't like her. All mothers adore their daughters, so I've always known there was something wrong with me. I'm tired of trying to do what's right, or what will make me loveable. I'm ready to be me, and if that includes snuffing out lives along the way, so be it.

"When we go out for this, I always want you in a skirt. Understand?"

"Why?" I ask while gazing at him, and he smirks.

"I need easy access to my sweet pussy, baby."

"Is that why you do it? It gets you off?"

He laughs as he cuts the ignition off.

Reaching over, he tucks the hair in my face behind my ear.

"Whenever you're around, it gets me hard. Watching you kill people, fuck yeah, it turns me on, baby. Me killing? No, it's not a sexual thing. It's more of a relief. When someone dies at my hands, it's beautiful to watch, and physically feels like I've been in excruciating pain, and in an instant, it evaporates."

I know there's something in Nico's past that hurts him, but I don't know what it is, and right now is not the time to ask. If I ask when he's planning to hurt people, he's going to take it as a judgment, and it's not. I just want to know him better. It's like a craving that won't go away. The desire to know him inside and out is powerful. Outside is easy, but inside, he keeps guarded. And I know, all his life he's been told there's something wrong with him, and I'm sure that's why he keeps certain things to himself. He once told me that I was the one person he didn't want to judge him, but to accept him as he is. I didn't in the beginning, but I do now. In time, he'll realize he has a safe space with me no matter what he says.

"Fuck, I love you. Let's go get a drink and take a look around."

I nod and move to open the door, and he growls at me.

"Fucking wait."

Removing my hand from the door, he shakes his head at me, gets out of the car and walks around to my door, and opens it.

Tilting my head at him, I say, "Reaper Bonetti, the gentleman."

"The gentleman," he repeats and then grins, "I think I prefer, 'The Pussy Killer'."

I get out of the car, and he takes my hand and pulls me against his side.

"You are to stay close to me. If you need to use the restroom, you'll tell me. I do not want you out of my sight, if at all possible. Understood?"

"Yes. Are you always so intense?"

We walk to the door and he answers me, "When it comes to you, yes, always."

I could remind him that, if I can kill people, I should be able to take care of myself. I've been doing it for a while now, but I know that doesn't make me invincible.

Chapter Thirty-Three
REAPER

Nobody will look at me and wonder why I'm not dead. My employees knew it was all a hoax. For the benefit of my girl. She needed to think I was gone. Once Bella thought I was dead, it was going to go one of two ways. I'd find her and take her again, or she'd realize, not only was she mine, but she wanted to be. I'm relieved it was the latter.

She stares at me with unasked questions, every time someone greets me with, 'Good evening, Mr. Bonetti, it's so good to see you.'

If Bella asks me, I'll answer regardless of how uncomfortable it is, but I don't think she has figured that out yet. We take a seat at a table with a chair on one side, and a booth on the other. Automatically, I take the booth, because I plan to keep my hands on her. I watch her as she glances around the club. First, she looks at the large black 'U' shaped bar, with no bar stools in front of it. My plan early on was to not have people congregating at the bar. Her gaze turns to the black round tables with silver chairs, and then the dance floor, where people are bumping and grinding relentlessly.

Originally, I thought this club would be used for money laundering in the family business, but I quickly found out it was part of my father's retirement plan for me. When he told me I was too unhinged for the mafia, I laughed because I thought he was joking, but he wasn't. He didn't say anything for a long time, but I've always believed he decided Psycho would not become the head of the family during the same time period. He was sick for a long time before he clued us in, and everything was already in place before he had the conversation with the three of us. Bones wasn't there, because he was the first to be notified. Bones is a pain in my ass, but it was probably the right decision. I think even Psycho knows that now. He isn't a leader. Not because he isn't strong enough, but because he's too much like me. My oldest brother tends to do whatever he wants to, without considering consequences. In the mafia, that's dangerous. It can wipe out entire families. Like a good boy scout, you need to always be prepared. While Psycho will set fires everywhere, regardless of who gets burned, Bones thinks more methodically, and has everything planned out, before he strikes.

The waitress brings over a whiskey and sets it in front of me, and asks Bella if she'd like to see the wine list. My girl crosses her arms over her chest, and narrows her gaze at Sheila, and says, "I'll have a whiskey. Just because I'm a girl, doesn't mean I can't handle hard shit."

The server looks from Bella to me with a concerned expression.

"Of course, I'm sorry."

The waitress leaves, and Bella turns to me.

"I choose her. Can we do her?"

I chuckle and whisper in her ear.

"Settle down, living dead girl. People are going to hear you and think you plan on fucking her. Also, my employees are off limits, because I would have to restaff my club, which I have no intention of doing."

She gazes at me with obvious shock on her face.

"Your club? You own this? I saw 'Bonetti' on the sign and knew your family owned it, but I didn't realize it was yours."

I nod. "That's right, baby. If you have a question, ask, and I'll tell you. We don't have secrets."

Once her drink is brought over, she takes a sip and says, "Isn't it bad for business to," she waves her hand in the air, "*you know*, the customers."

She's trying hard to not say kill, which is fucking adorable. In the crime world, my extracurricular activities are not a secret. My staff knows full well, but they also know I don't hurt employees. The customers are a mix, some know and some don't, but I think the majority wonder if it's a rumor, or fact. It says 'Club Bonetti' on the sign, so anyone that walks in here likely knows I'm from a mafia family. You would think people would be smart enough to stay away from a family that runs a criminal enterprise, but they don't. Somehow it has become a cool factor. What it boils down to is, people are fucking stupid.

I shrug my shoulders.

"People know this is owned by a member of a criminal family. Do you think they stay away for their safety? No, it makes them more interested in being here. And for every person that mysteriously disappears, another will replace them to spend money in my club."

"What about the," she mouths the word, "police?" silently.

I brush her hair out of her face, so I can look into those blue eyes that make my cock so hard it hurts.

"They don't work for the people, baby, they work for us. In the event that one of us gets caught up in something with some new detective, there's another five that make evidence disappear. It's always a possibility that things could get hairy, but it hasn't happened yet. A case never goes far because we make it go away, one way or another."

I take a gulp of my whiskey with my free hand, as I grip her waist harder than I need to.

She looks around the club at the different people.

"How do you decide?"

I watch her watching a pretty brunette from a distance. I know her. She fucked Kage, in this very club. Her name is Melissa, and she's attractive, but nothing like Bella.

"You want to see her die, don't you, living dead girl?" I whisper in her ear.

She nods slowly, without taking her eyes off Melissa.

"Do you see the man in the gray suit at the bar?"

She glances at the bar quickly, as the bartender hands the man a drink.

"That's her current boyfriend. He's a member of the Abruzzo family. You may remember his brother attacking you."

Bella turns her head to me and cocks it. My cock gets hard at the fire in her eyes, as she says, "I want them."

Bones would tell me to calm her down, because it will only escalate the situation with their family, but he is in my club, knowing what happened to his two brothers. Besides, whatever she wants, she should have. If it's in my power, I'll give it to her.

"Go talk to her, living dead girl. Invite her to the VIP area."

Bella looks at me with a horrified expression. "What?"

"You'll be fine. I won't take my eyes off of you. If we have to, we'll force them upstairs, but this is the easiest way."

She grabs my face aggressively, and kisses me hard, her tongue sliding around mine. I'm surprised, but fucking delighted, when she wraps her small hand around my throat and squeezes, restricting my breathing slightly. *Fucking intoxicating.*

Pulling back with a dangerous look in her eyes, she says, "I'll meet you upstairs."

I watch my beautiful girl walk over to Melissa. My eyes focus on Bella's ass, and the way it sways with perfection as she crosses the room.

I'm not sure what she was worried about, because instantly they are talking and laughing. Bella strokes Melissa's dark spiral curls between her fingers sweetly as they have a conversation I can't hear. Tony Abruzzo joins into their conversation, and my skin prickles. If he lays a finger on her, he'll never make it upstairs. I don't know about Melissa, but he'll never turn down an opportunity to go to the VIP floor, because he's never been allowed. I don't allow members of other families upstairs unless, of course, they aren't coming out alive.

She loops her arm with Melissa's, and I get up and follow after them, as they walk up the spiral staircase leading to the VIP room. I take two steps at a time, because having her out of my line-of-sight bothers me more than I can handle. The second I walk in, two things happen. The tingling in my neck returns, and Abruzzo looks at me like he's going to kill me. He wishes. I know he isn't armed, because only my family is allowed to have weapons here. Everyone is searched. They don't like it, but if they want to come in, there's not a choice.

"Reaper," he growls, attracting the attention of both women. Melissa gazes at me with wide eyes, causing me to chuckle. She knows she's in trouble, because after years of dating mafia men exclusively, she knows this isn't a good situation, with men from two opposing families, ready to face-off. She's what Kage refers to as a mafia whore. She fucks men involved in organized crime, because she wants to tie one down. Melissa doesn't give a fuck about them. It's all about both money and power. The two things that drive our families. Without both of those things, there would be no mafia.

Chapter Thirty-Four

Bella

I watch the two men closely. If he tries to hurt Nico, I'll lose it and kill him myself. No one will take him from me, I will not allow it.

Melissa grabs my arm. "We have to get out of here."

The room is large, with a massive booth to the left of the door, and a bar to the right, with two bartenders that are watching Nico closely. I'll have to ask him about the three stripper poles at the back later, but now is definitely not the time.

Nico watches Abruzzo with a look I've seen before. It's the one he had in the kitchen that terrified me, but this time it's not aimed at me. His eyes are black as coal, his stance wide and threatening, and I can almost see the tingling in his neck he told me about, and when his murderous tendencies aren't aimed at me, it's hot. *Really fucking hot.*

He points in the direction of the bar.

"Get out."

His staff do not need to be told twice. I'm assuming they've been through a similar situation before. They quickly leave and close the door behind them. Melissa decides she's had enough, and runs toward the door the staff left through, and I go after her, and drag her head back and slam it into the door. The thud is loud, as is her wail, as she falls to the floor.

I glance at Nico, and he grins at me and mouths, 'good girl'.

Abruzzo takes advantage of his attention being on me, and pulls back and cocks Nico in the jaw. The man known to the world as Reaper wraps both hands around his throat, and squeezes with crushing force.

"Wrong move, asshole."

Melissa sits on the floor, holding her hand to her bloody head, while she trembles from obvious fear. I'm close enough that she knows running is pointless. I will catch her.

It becomes clear how much stronger Nico is than me, because the man slumps to the ground within minutes. The second I witness him being safe, I push Melissa so that she's laying down, and climb on top of her, placing my hands around her throat.

Nico groans in the background, but this isn't enough for me. This is how he likes to kill, but I want blood, which has never happened before.

"Nico?"

"Yes, baby," he says as he steps beside me.

"Do you always do it this way? Don't you think her blood would be so beautiful?"

She whimpers as I squeeze her throat. Her eyes are wide, and the loveliest shade of green. I watch the pure terror in her expression, and Nico is right, it's fucking beautiful. Tears stream down her face and, while I know I should feel bad, I don't. Instead, every sense feels heightened. My hearing is crisp, my sight is sharper than ever before, and the feeling of her trembling body in my hands does things to me I don't recognize. It's different with him here. Or is it because she's a woman? I'm not sure, but it's powerful.

Nico holds a knife out for me.

"It'll make a mess."

He nods slowly. "Yes, living dead girl, it will. We have people to clean up such messes here now. Do whatever feels right. Let the darkness in. Let it consume you, guide you."

I take it from him, happy that he even trusts me with a blade after what happened. When I take my hand from her throat, she tries to scramble free, but screams loudly when I stab her in the chest, then the stomach, and finally I tilt her head back, and drag the blade across her throat. The blood pours from her neck. There's also blood coming from her other wounds, but not like this. Her green eyes quickly go from vibrant to dull, appearing glazed, cloudy, and it's beautiful. *Nico was right. About everything.*

Climbing off her, I turn to him and brush my hair out of my face with my free hand. He stares at the knife in my other hand and chuckles softly.

"I'm going to need you to put the blade on top of the bar, living dead girl."

"You don't trust me?" I ask because that feels like a gut punch, although I should understand, given what happened before.

He smirks at me before it turns to a grin.

"I trust you, Bella, but I don't think you understand what you did to me. I'm going to fuck you so hard, your head is going to spin, so please put the knife down, so I don't have to worry about hurting you."

Walking over to the bar, I place the knife down and glance at my fingers, which are covered in blood. I sniff at it and Nico growls at me.

"Don't even think about it, living dead girl. You want to be a sexy little vampire? You can taste mine. No one else's."

Stepping over to me, he grabs the side of my skirt and unzips it.

"I have a shirt you can change into, but not bottoms, so I don't want to get blood on it."

He moves back and I allow my gaze to travel down his body, and I smile when I see his hard cock pressing against his pants. Nico watches me, as he reaches behind his neck and pulls his shirt over his head. Why is that so hot?

I press my thighs closed, and he notices because he doesn't miss much.

"Is my pussy wet for me already?"

Returning my gaze to his, I admit, "Yes."

Kicking off his shoes, he doesn't take his eyes from mine as he undoes his jeans and removes them, before tossing them to the side of the room with the t-shirt.

He places his hand on my face and gently tilts my head back.

"You are fucking it for me, Bella. The most beautiful creature I've ever seen. A dark soul that matches mine. Dangerous, yet dainty. Almost everything can be broken, but I don't think you can be. Believe me, I tried. I'll never morph into a good man, but fuck, I'll be good to you. Only you. Like me, you're a killer. You have taken lives, but far more than that, you kill pain. You take the pain away, and make living not only bearable, but something I look forward to. I have never been afraid of death, but I am now, because I don't ever want to not feel this with you."

"Nico," I gasp.

He slides his hands in my hair, and tilts my head back, and runs his tongue up the length of my throat. Moving my head to the side, he bites my neck hard and growls.

"Mine. Forever."

"Yours," I gasp, as he licks and sucks his way all over my neck.

Grabbing my shirt at the sides, he rips it from my body. Taking my bra straps between his fingers, he pulls it down until my breasts are exposed, and he groans.

"So stunning. You take my breath away."

He hooks his thumbs into either side of my panties, and lowers them to the floor, and I step out of them.

Looking up at me, he has a serious expression on his face.

"I need you to be a good girl, and do exactly as you're told so you don't get hurt."

Running my hand through his hair, I say, "If you kiss me, I'll do anything you want me to, Nico. There are no limits. There is nothing I won't do for you."

He rises to his full height and takes my face in his hands.

"What I want is for you to join me in everything in life. I want you to join my family business with me. I need you by my side in all things."

"I'm not family."

156

He growls and slams his lips to mine, kissing me, biting at my lips, and digging his fingers into my scalp like he simply can't get enough.

Staring at me with heat, he says, "You are my family. You're my everything. If the requirement is for you to have the Bonetti name, you've got it. I'll marry you, the second I'm done fucking you."

I blink fast as I try to make sense of his words, but I'm sure I'm confused, because there's simply no way.

"You want to marry me? Is that what you're saying, Nico?"

Chapter Thirty-Five
REAPER

It never even occurred to me until tonight. Of course, I want her to be my wife. Isn't that what you do, when you're so fucking consumed by someone that you can't bear to be away from them for five damn seconds?

Dragging my thumb over her lips, I say, "You're the missing piece to my lonely black soul, so yes, that's what I'm saying. Marry me, and take away the pain."

Placing her bloody hands on my face, she stands on her toes and smiles softly.

"I'll marry you, Nico."

Sliding my hands to her head, I hold her firmly and tilt her head to the side, and kiss her like I'm going to devour her, and I've considered it. It's quick but aggressive. Pulling back, I order her, "Turn around, face the bar."

As always, when her ass is facing me, I dig my fingers into the letters spelling my name. This was something I decided, and simply did without putting much thought into it, but I don't regret it. Every time I see it, my heart fucking pounds.

I slide my hands up to her hips.

"I'm going to lift you, and you're going to hold on to the other side of the bar. Do not let go."

I pick her up and she does as she's told. Grabbing her thighs, I spread them and am instantly rewarded with the scent of her arousal. The smell that is only for me.

Standing behind her, I push into her with one hard thrust. I hold her legs in a bruising grip, she looks like she's flying, as I fuck her harder than I ever have.

Every little whimper is just for me.

Every scream is just for me.

Every fucking orgasm is for me.

The way she begs for more, she only does for me.

"Nico!" she screams as her upper body arches off the bar, and her pussy clenches down on my cock.

"Bend your legs and let go of the bar."

She does, and I pull out of her and turn her to her back, so I can see her beautiful face. With a smirk, I say, "Much better."

Pushing back into her, I groan at how fucking drenched she is. I fuck her as hard as I did before, but this time it threatens to take me apart over and over. She is so stunning on her back for me, her bra around her waist, and tits bouncing with every thrust. It's all perfect, but then she raises herself, places her elbows on the bar and stares at me, while I grip her thighs and pull back and push my hips forward, slamming into her. A dead girl's blood on her face shouldn't do to me what it does. My beautiful living dead girl looks feral for me, and I'll never not like it.

"Nico," she cries, as her head hangs over the side of the bar, and I lose myself in her. Holding her thighs tight, my abs tighten as I fill her with my cum, with a grunt.

"Sit up," I say, still breathing heavily, and wrap my arms around her and carry her to the shower on the other side of the room. My cock slips out of her as I set her on the floor, and start the shower. It's a much smaller space than the one in my house, but we'll make it work.

"What do we do with the dead people?"

I pull her under the water with me, and tilt her head back and wash the blood from her face.

"After we're done here, I'll call my brother and have him send someone to deal with it."

Is he going to be happy? Fuck no. I could easily take them to the graveyard and bury them there, but if he wants me to work for the family, he's going to pay the price. And this is part of it.

160

I wash her body, but her hands and arms bear the worst of it. Did she surprise me by wanting blood? Absolutely, but it was fucking magnificent. I told her to let the darkness in, and she did. Fuck, did she ever.

"Do you want kids?" she asks as I hold her in my arms, and the water falls over us.

I chuckle softly, because the idea of us having kids sounds ridiculous to me.

"You want a couple of tiny unhinged lunatics running around, baby?"

Between the two of us, I imagine they'd have to turn out to be at least as evil as we are. I don't think it'd be possible for them to be normal, and if they were, that'd really suck. Normal is boring.

"Maybe at some point, but not now."

I kiss her softly and tell her to finish up.

"I'll put a t-shirt on the counter for you. I'm going to dry off and get dressed, so I can call Bones."

Stepping out of the shower, I grab a towel off the hook and dry off, and then grab a shirt for her and put it beside the sink.

I walk out to get dressed, and glance at Tony and Melissa with a chuckle. After getting dressed, I fish my phone from the pocket of my jeans and call my brother.

"Reaper," he answers, sounding agitated before I tell him what we've done.

"Do you want the good news or bad news first?"

"Fuck," he growls in response, and then says, "Good. Let's get that out of the way, before I get a headache."

"I think I'll come to work for the family as requested, but I have some stipulations. I'll come talk to you tomorrow about it."

"It wasn't a fucking request, Reaper."

I chuckle and tell him the truth.

161

"There are two bodies in the VIP room of my club. The mafia whore Melissa, and her current boyfriend, Tony Abruzzo. I need someone to deal with it so I can take my girl home."

Then I add, "There's a substantial amount of blood, so make sure someone comes that can handle that."

I'm met with silence, which is rare for any of my brothers.

"Bones?"

"Were you attacked? You never make people bleed. That's Psycho's game, not yours."

"Well, Abruzzo hit me, but no, it wasn't me. My future wife did it."

He groans loudly, "Fucking living dead girl."

I grin with pride as he bitches at me.

"I swear to fucking God, Nico. It's supposed to be my own kids that give me gray hair, not my damn full grown brother. You're going to give me a full head of it before this baby is even born."

Bella walks out of the bathroom, and what a fucking vision she is, wearing the Club Bonetti t-shirt with my white logo over her left tit.

He lets out a long, drawn-out sigh.

"Is she a fucking serial killer too now?"

"It would appear so. Look, I gotta go, but I'll see you tomorrow," I answer.

He can bitch at me tomorrow, because right now I want to take Bella home, and fuck her until she's unconscious. Maybe even then.

Chapter Thirty-Six

Bella

I've been a wreck all morning, because the Bonetti brothers all have reason to hate me. I'm not worried about my safety, but I don't want his family to dislike me either. From what Nico has told me, it seems Bones has taken on a fatherly role within the family since their dad died. He is in charge, and it feels like my future is in his hands.

I didn't realize he was standing in front of me, but Nico lifts my chin in his hand, and tilts his head with concern.

"I've been saying your name for five minutes, Bella. What's going on inside your head?"

I stare into his gaze and admit, "They are going to hate me, Nico. I stabbed you."

He runs his free hand through his hair. We talked about this last night, so he's probably getting annoyed with me, but I can't change how I feel.

"Stop fucking saying that. You didn't stab me, if anything I stabbed myself. It wasn't intentional."

He sighs and sits on the couch beside me, and pulls me onto his lap, and places one hand on my back and the other on the back of my thigh.

"They weren't happy when I was injured, but they will learn to deal with it. They'll have to. At least you called Bones. You didn't leave me to die."

"What if he gives you an ultimatum, and makes you choose between me and your family, Nico?"

Understanding shows on his face, and I don't think he had even considered it before I said it.

"That's what you're worried about, baby?"

I nod slowly as tears roll down my cheek.

"The thought alone robs me of the air in my lungs, and I don't know how I'd possibly go on without you."

He shakes his head, like what I suggested is impossible.

"That is not going to be the outcome. I refuse to live without you, so either my brothers learn to accept us together, or they can fuck off. I've been the odd fucked up one, my whole life. There are so many things they don't even know about me, things that happened to me, that contributed to everything I am. One thing they do know though, is that I live my life on my terms, and no one dictates my choices. Believe me, they've tried. Nothing, and no one, will make me leave you."

"What happened to you, Nico?"

The pain in his eyes is almost too much to bear, but I don't look away. I stay with him, because whatever the answer to my question is, it changed him.

"Fuck," he says quietly, as he closes his eyes like it hurts to look at me, and he has never not wanted to see my eyes. I reach up and touch his face.

"You can tell me anything."

He sighs a shaky breath.

"I had an uncle. Frank. Fuck, I hate him. He convinced my father I was too weak for the mafia, because I was more emotional than men in the family are supposed to be. I was just a kid, but my dad agreed to let my uncle train me. To toughen me up."

He takes in a shaky breath, and it makes my chest hurt for him.

"You don't have to tell me. I'm sorry."

He opens his eyes and says, "I want to tell you. I've never spoken about this to anyone. My father was ashamed, so I kept it to myself, but I want you to know me, all of me. Even the disgusting parts."

I kiss his cheek softly.

"Take your time."

"For seven years, he beat me daily. It was part of what he called training. That was the easy part. Jesus Christ, I can't tell you the rest, Bella. You'll never look at me the same."

I take his face in my hands, the way he has done with me so many times.

"Nico, I love you. All of you, and nothing could make me love you less. Tell me or don't tell me, but don't keep it to yourself because you're afraid I'll think differently of you."

He stares at me with so much anguish in his expression, but he continues.

"I didn't lie to you when I said I was a virgin, but I also wasn't completely truthful. He fucked me frequently. When I was fourteen, my father came down to the basement, and found me lying naked in a pool of my own blood, with a lead pipe beside me. I had been beaten with it and fucked with it."

I shift myself so I'm straddling his lap, and wrap my arms around his neck, and hold him close to me. I'm horrified by his words, but I am careful not to show it, because I don't want him to think I view him in a bad light. I know this was very difficult to tell me, and my heart is shattered for him.

"You were not fucked, Nico. You were raped, as a child. Nothing you could've done would have made you deserve that. Nothing."

He presses his face into my neck, as he holds onto me like he might not make it, if I let go of him. I won't. Not ever.

"I love you, Nico, and it changes nothing for me. Although, I think we should kill your uncle."

He chuckles through his tears.

"My father sent him away, and then declared it would be a secret. I never saw him again. I don't know for sure if he's alive."

"Your brothers don't know?"

"No," he answers flatly.

Running my fingers through his hair, I kiss his forehead softly and he moans lightly, clearly appreciating my touch.

"Would Bones know?"

He clenches his jaw and bites.

"Bella, don't. Yes, he probably knows where he is, and no, we aren't going to ask him. He doesn't know, and he isn't going to. The only reason I didn't kill the asshole myself is because I'm too fucking weak. I can't stomach being in the room with him long enough to end his pathetic life, so let it go. This isn't why I told you."

"You're right. I'm sorry. Tell me what I can do for you. What do you need, Nico?"

"You," he growls, and grabs my shoulders and throws me down onto the couch.

Lifting my skirt, he cups my pussy and groans.

"This sweet little spot is the cure for whatever ails me. So, I'm going to fuck you, and then we're going to go deal with my annoying brother."

He places a hand beside my head on the couch, and unzips his jeans with his free one. With a sexy, gravelly groan, he pushes inside me.

I wrap my legs around his hips and my arms around his neck, pulling his delicious weight on top of me. Lifting his head, he slides his hand around my throat, and I whimper softly.

"Squeeze."

With a smirk on his sinful lips, he does as I ask and restricts my breathing, which intensifies everything.

It becomes too much and I claw at his hand, but he doesn't stop squeezing.

"Trust me, living dead girl. I could take your life away, but I won't, because you fucking give me life."

He stares into my eyes, and when he finally releases his hold on my burning throat, my orgasm slams into me, and I'm a screaming, crying, gasping mess.

Licking at my tears, he groans, "Beautiful. I once thought I wanted to watch you die, but bringing you close, over and over again, is fucking mesmerizing."

I reach my hand up and place it around his throat, and his eyes darken in response.

"That's right, living dead girl. Take everything from me."

He doesn't slow down as I squeeze, instead, he speeds up his thrusts at a vicious pace. I let go, and his head falls into my neck while he breathes hard against my skin, followed by a low throaty growl when he comes.

Chapter Thirty-Seven

REAPER

After I turned us over on the couch and had her on top of me, she fell asleep. I watched her for a long time before I joined her. Bella's warmth does that to me, frequently. She gives me peace unlike anything I've ever known. I wake to my phone ringing, and am immediately annoyed at whoever the fuck dares to interrupt my content state.

Grabbing it from my pocket, I groan when I see 'Bones' flash across the screen, as well as the time in the left corner. Fuck.

"Hey, asshole," he says when I answer.

"What, dickhead?" I respond, and his annoyance clearly trumps mine.

"Where the fuck are you?" He growls angrily, as Bella stretches on top of me. I wrap my arm around her back so she can't get up, because I need a few more minutes with her before everything turns to chaos.

"On my couch, with my dick inside my girl. Want a picture?"

I can hear him pacing, and I bite my lip to shut down the chuckle itching to get out.

"Are you coming or not?"

"Already did, but thanks for asking."

"Nico," he growls, and that's confirmation that he's truly pissed off.

"Athena is making dinner, and for some fucking reason, she cares if you're here."

"Alright, we'll be there soon."

My sister-in-law is my one soft spot, other than Bella. She went through fucking hell, not unlike myself, and she's a goddamn warrior. I like strong women, and she's made of steel. Bones knows damn well I'd never let her down.

I disconnect the call and smack Bella's ass.

"We need to go, before my brother loses what's left of his small mind."

She bites my neck hard.

"Ow! What the fuck?"

She climbs off me and giggles.

"Smack my ass, and I'll give it right back to you."

"Do you not like it?"

With a sassy little smirk, she says, "Very much, but I also like biting you."

This woman. I get up and fix my pants, grabbing my t-shirt and putting it back on while Bella smoothes out her skirt, takes her hair down, and puts it back up. I don't know how she does it, but she makes a fucking basic ponytail look elegant.

"Do you think we smell like sex? Maybe we should shower first."

I chuckle. "That's my favorite scent, baby. Besides, we don't have time. Athena is making dinner."

She rolls her eyes.

"Fanfuckingtastic. We aren't just going to talk with three men that hate me, but sitting through a meal with them as well. Oh, I know! Maybe she'll hate me too, so there can be an extra person that wants me dead."

I grab her hands and pull her with me.

"Let's go, so you can see it's not as bad as what you've built it up to be, inside that pretty head of yours," I say, and really hope I'm not lying to her because, honestly, I don't really know. Psycho won't give a shit either way, and Kage will be his normal asshole self, but Bones is a wild card. If he thinks us being together is bad for business, or that she's a threat in general, it may very well be an uphill climb.

170

We walk through the house and outside to my waiting Range Rover, and I pull her into my arms and kiss her on the forehead.

"I promise you, everything will be okay. I can't tell you not to worry because you will anyway, but I swear to you, nothing bad will happen."

She presses her face against my chest and whispers, "I love you."

"I love you too, living dead girl. Let's get this over with."

Opening the door for her, she gets in, and I walk around to the driver's side and get in. I know she's concerned that something my brothers could say might change things between us, but it's fucking impossible. Bones will probably be pissed about the bodies, but I don't think he'd ever ask me to leave her, because while he's an asshole, he wants me to be happy. Like Kage said, this is the most normal thing I've ever done.

As I drive, she sits staring out the window, and it's like she isn't even here.

Reaching down, I grab her leg, and she jumps.

"Goddamn it, Bella, stop. It's going to be fine."

"Sorry," she says quietly.

Removing my hand from her leg, I let her be, because I know the only way to set her mind at ease is to simply do this, and be done with it.

Continuing to stare out the window, she speaks so softly I wonder if I'm even meant to hear it.

"Every boyfriend I've ever had leaves me, because I'm not good enough. Number two and three were because their families didn't approve of me. What kind of a girl isn't even liked by her own mother? If that isn't a red flag, I don't know what is. So I hear you when you say everything will be fine, but I know better. Tonight, your brothers will take you to the side, and tell you I'm not what you need, and maybe they'll be right. Maybe I'll get lucky and one of them will cut my heart out of my chest, so I don't have to feel myself dying without you."

All the air leaves my lungs, as I pull the car over. My chest fucking aches. I've never spent the time to really find out what her life has been like, and this revelation fucking guts me. There's more than one way to abuse a child, and suddenly I feel like she's been through more than she let on. Maybe she didn't get her ass fucked with a lead pipe, but she's been hurt. Really fucking hurt.

"Get over here, Bella. Now."

When she climbs onto my lap, I wrap my arms around her and hold her tight.

"Let me be really fucking clear with you, baby. Even if Bones told me to leave you, I wouldn't. I'd much prefer to cut my own fucking heart out, than live a single day without you. We are intense, fucked up, and perfect together. I don't want to have to make that choice, but if I'm put into that position, I'll choose you. Every fucking time, you'll be my choice. For me, you're not only good enough, you're more than enough."

She clutches onto my shirt and sighs audibly.

"I'm sorry. I don't know what's wrong with me. I'm so fucked up."

Running my fingers through her hair, I say, "You're perfectly fucked up, baby. If anybody says you're not what I need, they're wrong. Just be yourself, and anybody that can't handle it can fuck themselves. Maybe just don't kill anyone tonight."

With her head laying on my shoulder, she giggles, her breath washes over my neck, and of course, my cock gets hard, and she wiggles her sexy ass on my lap.

"Get back in your seat. I'll fuck your ravenous pussy the second we get home."

I've always heard it's the man that wants to have sex the most, not women, but with her, I'm not sure that's true. She makes comments about me killing her pussy, but she wants it as much as I do. It's just one of many reasons this woman will be my wife.

Chapter Thirty-Eight
BELLA

Nico takes my hand and walks me to the door. He glances at me, and pulls my hand to his lips and kisses my palm softly.

"Let's start with breathing, shall we?"

A very pregnant woman opens the door, with an ear-to-ear grin, and when she throws her hands around Nico's back, it's clear she must be Athena. The grumbling man behind her must be Bones. I saw him at the graveyard once, but I didn't get a good look since I was running for my life. He is handsome like Nico, but his hair is a lighter color. He's wearing a black dress shirt and matching pants, but I notice the skulls tattooed on his hands. The most notable thing about his appearance is the scowl on his face.

"Get your fucking hands off my wife."

Nico turns to him. "Hey, Dick."

"If you're going to work for the family, you'll need to learn some respect," he says as we step inside.

Nico smirks at him. "Mr. Dick? Sir Dick? Dick Sir?"

The woman smacks him in the chest and giggles. "Reaper, behave. Don't get him wound up, because I'm the one that will have to deal with it."

He grins in response and says, "Athena, this is Bella. Bella, this is my favorite sister-in-law, Athena, and her dickhead husband, Bones."

I grab his arm. "Nico, stop."

"Fine."

He turns to his brother. "Where are Kage and Psycho?"

Standing in the living room, Bones places his hand on his wife's stomach in a sweet way, and somehow I know it's at odds with how he is with anyone else.

"In the office, join them, and I'll be right there."

Nico kisses me on the cheek.

"I'll see you in a bit, baby. Trust me, you'll love Athena."

He walks up a spiral staircase as I watch him, and feel insecure, as Bones stares at me with what I've decided looks exactly like Nico's death eyes. Walking over to me, he narrows his gaze at me, while he crosses his arms over his chest.

"I hear you've taken up the hobby of killing people, like my little brother."

Nodding silently, I don't say more, because I know better. Something about him tells me you only speak when spoken to in his presence, and Nico is out of earshot.

"Let me be clear, living dead girl."

I shudder at the way he says Nico's nickname for me. It's nothing like when Nico says it, and I don't like it.

"If you touch one hair on my wife's head, I guarantee you, I will break every fucking bone in your body. When you beg for death, I'll break them all again. Do we understand each other?"

His wife gasps beside me. "Luca."

Raising my gaze, I glare back at him. He doesn't know me, but I don't like being threatened.

"I love your brother, and I'm not so disrespectful to come into his brother's home and hurt his family. Think what you want about me, but I'm not the monster you've decided I am. If you'd prefer, I can wait for Nico in the car."

"Nonsense!" Athena interjects.

"Luca, you go to your meeting, and I'll be fine here with Bella. If Reaper says she's safe, then she is. He would never put me in danger."

He kisses her quickly.

"I can have security here, just in case."

She shakes her head. "Luca, stop. Please."

After he kisses her again, he walks away and joins the other men in his office.

"Sorry about that. He's a little much with my safety, and it's gotten worse since I got pregnant."

She takes my hand and pulls me further into the living room, and to the sofa, and we both sit. They say pregnant women glow, and she really does. Athena has long dark hair, and pretty blue eyes that immediately remind me of Nico, which might sound disturbing, but I am careful not to compliment her on them.

"Luca says he thinks things are serious between you two. Are they?"

I nod with a smile.

"They are."

She claps her hands excitedly.

"I'm so happy. Reaper is a loving man, even though he doesn't see it. I've known since I met him. Because of the things he does, people think he only has darkness in his heart, but I'm guessing you also know that's not the case."

I smile as I think about him.

"He is my entire world, and I don't think I could survive without him."

Athena rubs her belly, as she stares down and smiles at the life inside her.

"I saw the way he looked at you. I don't think you need to be worried about being without him."

"When are you due?"

She giggles softly.

"Six weeks, and I can't wait to get this baby out."

Suddenly, loud voices travel from upstairs, followed by heavy footsteps. I look up and see a furious glare on Nico's face. He storms toward me.

"Bella. Now. We're leaving. Athena, I'm sorry."

I get up and walk over to him to ask what's going on, when the other three come down the stairs. Bones growls, "Goddamn it, Reaper. We aren't done."

Nico gives him the same growl back.

"We are done. Fuck you. Fuck this family. I'm done!"

I glance at Bones, and his expression is full of pain. It's heartbreaking, even if I don't know what's going on.

"I didn't fucking know."

Nico takes my hand in his, and tightens his hold around mine painfully, pulling me to the door as Bones' loud voice booms through the entryway.

"I didn't fucking know!"

Without turning around, Nico says, "I'm a Bonetti in name only. You have two brothers now. Leave me alone."

Taking a look back, I see Athena standing with her hand over her mouth like she's horrified, and I agree with her, although I don't know why.

Whatever happened in there is going to change everything.

Chapter Thirty-Nine
REAPER

Three days later...

"Do you want me to go, Nico?"

I glance up at a Bella I've never seen before. She still looks like the same stunning woman I've gotten to know, but she's different. Unsure. I don't have to ask why, because I already know the answer. I've been an asshole for the last three days. I've barely talked to her, and I haven't touched her once. She was my peace. My goddamn healing source, but I pushed her away because, as usual, I can't deal with my emotions. The voices in my head are so loud they nearly echo.

"No."

"I don't know how to reach you. It feels like I'm losing you, and it scares me."

Blowing out a deep breath, I say, "Come here."

She walks over to me, and I pull her onto my lap.

Wrapping her arms around my neck, she lays her head on my shoulder, and lets out a shaky breath.

"You don't have to battle your demons alone."

As I stroke my fingers through her hair, the first sense of peace I've had in days fills me.

"I'm sorry."

Lifting her head up, she kisses my neck, before laying it back down.

"Will you tell me what happened?"

"Bones wants to let Frank back into the family. He has done well on his own, and he thinks he's an asset. I told him what he did to me and then left. I think he knew."

"Oh, Nico," she says, as she lifts her hand and runs her fingers through my hair.

"Are you sure? Did he say something that made you think that?"

"No. I can't explain it well, but when he told me his plans, it felt like a punch to the gut. Like he was trying to punish me for being such a pain in the ass."

She sits up and gazes into my eyes. "You should talk to him, Nico. He's your brother. We're not all given a family that cares about us. If he knew, and still did that, then yes, you should never speak to him again. But Nico, what if he didn't?"

I open my mouth to respond, but am interrupted by the doorbell and instantly I know it's one of my brothers, because nobody else can get beyond the gate. Bella climbs off my lap, and I run a hand through my hair as I go to open the door.

Kage stands in front of me, with a look I've never seen on his face. I look around him to see if he's alone.

He shakes his head.

"It's just me."

I nod and say, "Come in."

We walk to the living room, and Bella says hello to him.

"I'll give you two some time. Do you mind if I use your laptop, Nico?"

Kissing her quickly, I say, "Help yourself."

I sit on one end of the couch, and Kage takes a seat on the other.

"Bones is pretty fucked up about what you said. We didn't know, man. Fuck, if we did, we would've killed him. Maybe dad couldn't bring himself to kill his own damn brother, but we would have."

Leaning back in the seat, I rest my head against the wall.

"I reacted. This was something I never planned to tell any of you, and when he said he was considering letting him back into the family, and the business, I exploded."

He nods. "I get it. Fuck, I wish someone would've told us. We were told you had a bad stomach bug, and that's why you were in the hospital."

Turning towards him, I say, "Dad told mom it was not to be spoken about, and you know she always listened to what he said. Speaking of, has anyone heard from her?"

He shakes his head with a chuckle.

"She's still on that cruise. The Caribbean, I think. Bones said she's supposed to be back before the baby is born."

Kage looks at me, and I know his next words will make him uncomfortable.

"Look, man. I am not good with feelings. I'm probably the worst out of the four of us, but you were a kid. It wasn't your fault. What happened to you is fucked up. You don't get to decide you aren't our brother, because you always will be. This is your way, Reaper. You hurt, and you shut everyone out that you can't kill."

He groans loudly. "Alright, I'm done. That's my maximum capacity for emotional conversation."

I chuckle at him.

"Bones sent you for this shit?"

"Well, he didn't think you'd open the door for him, so that left me and Psycho. He was afraid one of you would end up dead, because neither of you assholes think shit through."

I can't disagree with him. Psycho and I have both always been loose cannons.

He grins wide, like a little boy that's so proud of himself.

"So, how'd I do? Pretty good, right?"

I shake my head and laugh.

"Pretty good for a dickhead."

He rises from the sofa and asks, "Are you gonna be okay?"

I stand to walk him out, and shrug.

"I'll be fine. I'll kill a few people, and be back to myself."

179

"You're going to be the sole reason we have to repopulate the earth. Where do I sign up for that job?"

I laugh at him as he steps outside.

"You're an idiot, you know that, right?"

Running his hand across his jaw, like he's thinking about it, his face turns serious.

"Do me a favor and call Bones, alright? He's a mess, thinking we lost our brother."

I nod, and head back inside to find Bella.

When I enter the bedroom, she quickly closes the laptop.

Arching an eyebrow, I ask, "Hiding something, living dead girl?"

"Of course not," she says a little too quickly, but I choose to let it go, because she's with me all the time and if she's up to something, I will find out.

"You look better," she says, as she sets my laptop on the table beside the bed.

I nod as I walk over to her, ready to pounce on my pretty little prey.

"Nico?" she asks, but doesn't get a response.

Grabbing the hem of her shirt, I growl, "Hands up."

Once her hands are in the air, I pull the shirt over her head, revealing a light pink lacy bra. I quickly drop the shirt to the floor, and pull her bra straps down, and groan at the sight of her full tits.

I yank her cotton pants down and she stumbles backward, landing on the bed.

Hooking my thumbs into her panties, I pull them down too, until she's exactly as I want her. *Naked.*

"Get comfortable, and show me how you played with my pussy on the grave."

"Nico," she gasps, "No."

Pulling my own shirt off, she stares at me with the same hunger I feel for her.

After I get out of my pants, I stroke my cock, and she licks her lips while she watches me with such intensity, that I know she'll do anything I want her to. *Good little slut.*

Chapter Forty

BELLA

"Spread those pretty thighs for me."

Once I do, he climbs on the bed between my legs, and strokes his cock slowly, while his gaze travels my body as if it can devour me.

"Do you want this cock, living dead girl?"

"Yes," I whimper, because I do want him. The last three days without being connected to him have been torture. He has been close, but so far away, and I miss him like this.

Looking down at me, he smirks, and says, "Show me."

"It'll be weird, and very not sexy," I complain.

He chuckles softly.

"No, baby, you're wrong. It'll be the sexiest thing I've ever seen. That night at the graveyard, I watched you fall apart, but I couldn't see you as well as I wanted to. Tonight, I have a front row seat, and I want this so bad I can taste it. Please, baby, give it to me. Freely."

Taking a deep breath, I reach my hand between my legs, and touch my clit lightly.

"Fuck," he murmurs, "That's it. Such a good girl."

My gaze moves from his body, slowly taking in his sculpted physique, the eyeball tattoo that once confused me, to his defined abs, and finally his cock, that is weeping for me. Nico fists his length as his breaths get heavier, and it's the sexiest thing I've ever seen. My pussy pulses with need, as I slide two fingers inside me with my free hand.

"Jesus, baby. You're so hot like this. I can hear how wet your pussy is. Beautiful."

"Nico, I need you."

With his free hand, he digs his fingertips into my thigh, and groans, "I need you too, baby. Come for me, so I can have you."

Pressing down on my clit, I rub harder, trying to get there so I can have the only thing I want. *Him.*

He stares into my eyes, and it's powerful, because no man has ever looked at me the way he does. There's nothing I wouldn't do for him. Nico has captured every part of me, body, mind, and soul. He has completely consumed me, and I wouldn't change it if I could. My gaze drops to his hand, and I watch him fuck his hand for me. He slides in and out of his palm, with the occasional groan, that sets me on fire. It's watching him that finally pushes me over the edge. My body trembles as I moan his name repeatedly.

Quickly, he grabs my wrist, removing my fingers from my pussy, and brings them to his face. He inhales my scent with a growl.

"Feed me your cum."

He swirls his tongue over my fingers and between, not wanting to miss a drop and, while it's filthy, it makes me pulse with need all over again. He places his hands on the backs of my thighs, and pushes them apart, as he stares at my most intimate area.

"There's never any shame between us, Bella. Whatever the fuck I want, you'll give it to me, and I'll do the same for you in return. This pussy is fucking beautiful. You're mine to desecrate, and to cherish. I'll defile you, but also love the fuck out of you."

"Nico," I whisper as he pushes inside me. Sex is supposed to feel good, but this is on another level as it always is with him, but three days without this makes it even more so. He pulls his hips back, and slides back into me with a groan. His thrusts are slow and measured, like he's trying to control himself. Readjusting his position, he places a hand on either side of my head, and stares into my eyes, less than an inch from my face.

"Take my breath away."

Lifting himself slightly, he wraps his hand around my throat, as he runs his tongue along his bottom lip.

"My pleasure. I'll gladly drag you to the brink of death, only to bring you back to me, because you are the air in my lungs."

He speeds up his thrusts, slamming into me over and over again, as he squeezes his hand around my throat.

"Good girl," he groans, "Die for me."

Dots dance in my vision, as he cuts off my air, and instinctively I attempt to get free from his hold, but I can't. The dizziness is overwhelming, and he releases his hand, allowing me to gasp huge gulps of air as my body convulses with pleasure. I open my mouth, a strangled scream escaping from me, as my pussy clenches his cock and my back arches off the bed.

Nico grabs my hair, pulling hard as he slams his lips to mine, and grunts into my mouth. His tongue tangles with mine as he spasms inside me, causing me to moan in response. Our sounds are muffled by our combined mouths. This is how it's meant to be between us. Our bodies physically joined, as our hearts and minds are. He once said I was the missing piece to his soul, and that describes us perfectly. All my life, I've wandered the earth feeling lost. Like I was missing something. I never knew it was another person, but I do now. Nico would slaughter the entire planet to protect me, and I will do the same for him.

He rolls to his side and takes me with him, in a tight embrace.

"I need to buy you a ring."

I giggle as I place my leg over his hip.

"Nico, I don't need a ring."

Taking my hand, he lifts it to his mouth, and kisses my ring finger.

"You do. Every man will know you're mine, and if they even fucking look at you, they're dead."

I narrow my gaze at him. "Nico, people have eyeballs."

He chuckles softly.

"I can fix that."

"You're insane."

He grins wide, and it makes my heart pound when he looks so happy, when I know that hasn't always been the case.

185

"I know I am, baby. That's why we're perfect for each other. If one of us were normal, this wouldn't work."

"What's normal?" I ask, because I honestly am not sure if I even know.

He makes a face like he bit into a sour lemon.

"Boring. Going to work every day, dealing with people's stupid shit. Not craving bringing people to their death, I suppose."

"Weird," I say, and he chuckles.

"We're doing God's work really, because there are too many people. One trip to any public place will tell you that. There are too many fucking people."

I run my fingers over his chest to his shoulder, and trace the intricate eyeball tattoo on his skin. Not so long ago, it scared me, but now I find it fascinating. After three days of him getting almost no sleep, he closes his eyes, and his breathing gets heavier.

I whisper almost inaudibly.

"I'm sorry, baby. I have to do this, and I hope one day you understand. If the roles were reversed, you'd agree. I'll miss you, but hopefully if things go my way, I'll be back in your arms soon. I love you, Nico."

I kiss his lips softly, slowly removing myself from his arms, and climbing off the bed. Loving someone doesn't mean looking the other way when someone has hurt them. While I understand why he can't do it, I can. If I get killed in the process, I'm okay with it, but I can't continue to live in a world where a monster that destroyed him lives. Vengeance will be the most beautiful thing I've ever experienced, tainted only by Nico not being with me.

Glancing back at him one last time, after I'm dressed, with two knives in my sheaths on each thigh, I hold my hand to my heart.

If I die tonight, find me in the afterlife, because I'll be waiting for you to make me whole again

Chapter Forty-One
REAPER

Before I even open my eyes, I reach for her, and come up empty. Forcing my still tired eyes open, I find her side of the bed vacant. I groan with irritation, but get up and toss on some boxer shorts to go find her. I should spank her sexy ass for leaving my bed cold without her, and I just might, the second I find her.

Walking downstairs, I notice it's quiet, almost as if she isn't here, but I know that can't be the case. Maybe she fell back to sleep on the couch. I take a look in the living room and she isn't there either. When I make it to the kitchen, there's still no sign of her, except for a handwritten letter on the counter.

My Dearest Nico,

I have some things to take care of. Dangerous things, but things that need to be handled, regardless. As always, I promise to be as safe as I can be, but know I am only doing what has to be done. I carry you in my heart wherever I go, and I expect you to do the same. This time with you has been wonderful, life changing. If I don't come back, please know I tried. There is no scenario where I wouldn't. I didn't leave you, I'm just righting some wrongs. Fingers crossed, I'll see you soon, to get the spanking I have no doubt you'll think I deserve.

I love you, Nico.

Always and forever,

~ Living Dead Girl

I trace my fingers over her beautiful writing, as I try to figure out the absolute mindfuck of a riddle she left me. What the fuck is she even talking about? After reading it five times, I still don't know where she went, and I don't fucking like it one bit. All the hairs stand up as my neck begins to tingle. If someone hurts her, I'll slaughter everyone in sight.

Think, Nico, think.

Grabbing my phone off the island, I call Bones, unsure of what to do, but honestly, I haven't spoken to him since I told him we weren't family anymore, so it may not go my way.

"Reaper," he answers quietly, like maybe Athena is still sleeping.

"She's gone."

I talk to him while carrying the letter upstairs, to see if I can find out what she's been up to on my laptop.

"Did you have a fight?"

"No, just the opposite. Everything was perfect. Then I woke up to this fucking letter."

Opening my laptop, I see it was never turned off, and I remember her closing it when I came into the room. I should've gone with my gut, and found out what she was up to. Had I, she'd probably be here now, instead of putting herself in harm's way.

I read him the letter, and he's quiet afterward, as I stare at the picture of my uncle's house on the screen. Running my keystroke program, I see that she was searching the area, directions, as well as contacting a fucking drug dealer. What the absolute fuck? I'm not going to spank her, I'm going to beat her ass until she's black and blue. But of course, I have to find her first.

"Bones?"

"Yeah," he responds softly.

"She went to find Frank."

I hear him walking, and then he says, "Is she a fucking idiot? Jesus Christ, this is bad, Reaper."

188

Nobody knows what Frank is capable of more than I do, so I don't need him to tell me how bad this is.

"Get over here. I'll call Kage and Psycho. We are going to need all hands on deck. I don't have to tell you how dangerous he is, and I assume you're attached to this girl."

My voice comes out as low and broken as I feel at this moment.

"I can't fucking breathe without her, Bones. I don't even want to."

"You helped me save my woman, and I'm going to help you save yours. This is what family does."

I know my brother is angry with me, and maybe he has a right to that, but at the moment I can't deal with it. There can be nothing I focus on other than finding Bella.

"I'll see you soon," I say as I disconnect the call.

Aside from my family, there has been nothing I've given a fuck about for my entire life. She's the only stability I've ever known, and the short time she's been gone has me feeling like I'm unraveling. My chest hurts as an emptiness fills me. My sweet girl wants to make Frank pay for what he did to me, but she has no idea what she's walking into. He is the most evil man I've ever known. And if he gets the upper hand, and he likely will, death will be a walk in the park compared to what he does to her.

She knows how to fight, and is surprisingly skilled at taking normal lives, but mafia men are anything but normal. We are born into a violent criminal world, and are raised with it.

As bad as enduring his torture was, this is worse. Life with Bella made every ounce of pain worth it. If I'm left with nothing, my life may as well end, because it's all meaningless.

I get dressed quickly, and grab my keys to go to my brother's house. We know where she is. That's not a mystery, but will we get there before or after he kills her, that's the question that causes the lump in my throat to grow.

Chapter Forty-Two
BELLA

I'm not entirely sure what I expected, but when I arrive at his compound, I am surprised by the number of armed men standing around. It looks like the goddamn swat team is here. Yet, I know it's not the police, it's the mafia. Chances are fairly good that this is a suicide mission, but I won't back down. This is for Nico. My intention was to sneak onto the property, but a quick scan tells me that is not an option.

Walking up to the black gate that surrounds the property, I see it's open, but simply walking through is impossible, due to the man with a machine gun standing in front of it. I go up to him, and place my hand over my heart and gaze up into his eyes.

"My, you're tall," I say sweetly.

I bat my eyelashes at him slowly, and his lips lift into a smirk.

"How can I help you, sweetheart?"

Tilting my head slightly, I say, "I'm here to see Mr. Bonetti. He paid for the night."

"Another day, another whore. That man has a problem. Go on in."

Stroking my fingers down his chest, I smile, "Can you make sure the men with guns don't hurt me? You seem like the protective type. And guns scare me."

Pressing a button on his earpiece, he says, "Lower your weapons. Bonetti's whore is coming through."

Again, I give him my sweetest smile, which of course, is completely fake.

"We prefer sex worker. People don't say whore anymore, because it's offensive. The more you know," I say in a sing-song voice, as I skip through the gate.

Fucking asshole. I would've liked to kill him first, but I know better. He's heavily armed, and my key to getting in without being riddled with bullets. Maybe another day. I smile to myself as I pass more guards. There are six men on either side, and one nods to me.

"Go on in, Miss. He's waiting for you."

I paste a fake grin on my face and say thank you, but suddenly I'm nervous. Did they tell him I'm here? If he isn't actually expecting a girl to be here, I could be in trouble. And if one shows up after me, things might actually be worse. Fuck.

Calm your nerves, Bella. You've got this.

But then I wonder, what if I don't?

Shaking that thought out of my head, I approach the door. This was my decision, and some things are worth dying for. Some people are, and Nico is one of those people.

I open the door and walk into the mansion. There's a large entryway, with a crystal chandelier on the ceiling, and a bearskin rug in front of the fireplace to the left, with two large chairs that are empty. My heart is racing as I walk forward. This place is huge, and I have no idea where I'll find him, but I will. There's a set of stairs in the distance, but I decide to clear the lower level first, and then I'll go up there if I haven't located him.

To my left is an empty kitchen, with expensive looking, stainless steel appliances, and an island that makes me remember Nico's, and causes my chest to squeeze. I miss him already. I spot the gun sitting on the island, and quietly enter to retrieve it. It never hurts to have extra weapons, assuming it's loaded.

Making my way to the other end, I stop in the dining room, dead in my tracks, when I see an older gentleman sitting at the large oval dark wood table.

"You found me," he says with a stoic expression. "Are you a thief?"

I shake my head no.

His gaze travels the length of my body.

"Well, you don't look like a whore, but I'll be happy to make you one."

He's a good looking man, that reminds me a lot of Nico. Frank has a lot of the same characteristics in his face; his nose, and lips, look similar, and even his eyes, but they are like the death eyes I've seen on Nico. Not the kind ones. His hair is silver, but was probably dark at some point, before aging took hold of him.

"You need to pay for what you did to Nico. And I'm here to collect your debt."

He smiles at me, but it doesn't reach his eyes, it's probably not even possible.

"I assume you mean Reaper? You do know he's a violent man, right? What's a pretty girl like you doing getting herself tangled up with him?"

Picking up his crystal glass that looks like it has scotch in it, he takes a sip and sets it back on the table calmly.

"His violence is all because of what you did to him."

He shrugs like what he did is no big deal, and it infuriates me, but I need to keep myself calm like he is, or I'll get myself killed. Think like Nico would.

"Thank you. I like to think I had something to do with the lethal man he has become, as opposed to the pussy he was as a boy."

Raising an eyebrow, I say, "You raped him, you sick son of a bitch."

He shakes his head in denial, which only angers me further.

"My dick never touched that boy."

Is he for real? Does he actually believe, because he raped him with something else, that he didn't violate him?

"Doesn't matter. He was a child. How dare you?"

He takes another gulp of his drink, and pours more from a fancy decanter.

"I assume you aren't from a mafia family?"

"No," I answer, but I don't think that matters.

He chuckles softly.

"I didn't think so because if you were, you'd know what a mistake it is coming into a mafia man's house, planning to what? Hurt me? Let me give you a tiny lesson of the criminal world. We raise our boys to be lethal. Violent. They must be to survive in this environment. Nico was always different from the others. Maybe he had too much of his mother's DNA, I don't know, but he was soft. Always so deep in his feelings over something. My brother asked me to toughen him up, and I did. Look at him now. The boy kills people for sport. Perhaps you don't agree with my methods, but they worked. I think that is something we'd both agree on. Although, I do wonder what kind of man would send a woman to do a man's work. Maybe he's still the pussy he was as a child."

"He didn't send me. Nico is stronger than you'll ever be."

His small smile turns into a wicked grin.

"Reaper doesn't know you're here, does he? Which means, I have you all to myself."

Rising from his seat, he goes to the curio cabinet on the other side of the room, and pulls out a drawer and retrieves something I can't see.

Holding the gun up and aiming it at his head, I prepare to shoot, and he chuckles.

"I can see your reflection in the glass, whore. Go ahead and fire it. It's empty."

I pull the trigger anyway, and it clicks, but it's empty. He wasn't lying to me.

Turning to me, he holds a lead pipe.

"This is what I used on your Nico. And now I'll use it on you."

Chapter Forty-Three

REAPER

Looking up her location on her tracker confirmed my suspicions that she was at Frank's house. I'm not sure why I didn't think of looking there to begin with, but I know now, I was right. She's doing this for me, the one thing I never would've asked her to do, because this is not what I want. Not that I have any problem with her wishing him dead, or even killing him, but she's putting herself in so much danger. I believe in my girl and she is capable of many things, but taking on Frank alone is not one of them. Of course, I want her to prove me wrong, but I know for a fact that I'm about to lose the only thing that means anything to me. I was tempted to go straight there to try to get her, but I'm currently trying to think like Bones, and if I run in there like she did, I'll only get us both killed.

After getting out of the car, I walk the few steps to my brother's door and open it. I know he's waiting for me, and the other two if they aren't here yet. As soon as I walk in, Athena throws her arms around me.

"I'm sorry, Reaper."

"Me too," I respond, and I make my way across the great room to the stairs. I know Bones will be in his office, already working on intel. Before we arrive at the house, he will want to know who is there, entry points, and any possible complications. This is why my father chose him for the job. We joke around and give each other a hard time, but I know all of my brothers have my back, and there is no one I trust more than Bones to help me get Bella, and keep us all alive in the process.

Opening the door, I walk in and find a packed room. All three of my brothers are seated on the couch, as well as some faces I don't know. I arch an eyebrow at Bones, silently asking for an explanation.

"Have a seat," he says, as he runs a hand through his hair.

My brother is worried. He has nerves of steel, so I know he's found something out that isn't good.

"Again, I have to ask you, how serious are you about this girl, Reaper?"

As my heart drops, I fear the worst. He's not going to help me, and if he isn't, I'll go it alone, but chances are I will die.

"As serious as the fucking heart attack I feel like I'm having."

I stare at my brother dead in the eyes.

"She's my Athena. Could you go on without your wife? Because I really don't think I could breathe a single breath in a world where Bella doesn't exist."

He nods his understanding, with his arms crossed over his chest, from behind his desk, then clears his throat. "Then we're doing this. You should know what we're up against though."

A short man stands up next to Domenic De Luca, who I have met, but don't know well. They look comical because Domenic is a giant, and this man is petite, probably not more than five-foot-five.

"Hello, Mr. Bonetti. I work for the De Lucas, in Intel. I have been asked to gather information, so I will share with you what I have. Not long after your father cast your uncle from the family, he went with information to the Abruzzos. He is under their protection, and they know your girl is in the house with him. Any attack will not be a surprise one. They are most definitely expecting you."

"Fuck," I say, because what else can be said?

Bones looks at me and shakes his head.

"And this is why it's a bad idea to kill rival families over parking spots. A fucking parking spot. We could have potentially negotiated to get your girl out safely, but with three dead Abruzzos, that's not even worth attempting."

I drag my hands down my face.

"I'm sorry."

Domenic glances at me and says, "My brothers will be here shortly. We have your back on this, but I expect the same of your family in the future, should we need it."

Bones tosses back a drink I'm not sure he should be having, but I don't dare say a word.

"You know we always have your back, Domenic. Any De Luca that needs us and we'll be there. The Abruzzos have needed to be wiped out for a long time. My brother has simply moved that to the top of my to do list. All guards are Abruzzo guards, so they are to be killed on sight. The only person in that house that survives is my brother's girl. If there are other women there, kill them, I don't give a fuck, but the blue-eyed blonde had better live, if she's alive when we get there. Understood?"

If she's alive.

His words bounce around my head, and make me physically ill, because I know there's a good chance she may already be dead. This may be a recovery mission, and my chest squeezes tightly from that thought alone. If I have to see her dead with my own eyes, I'll never recover from it. It's ironic since that's exactly what I planned, to kill her, but now the thought of it is debilitating.

I want to think of her beautiful eyes, that soft smile she only gives me, the way she makes every part of me come to life, but right now all I can think about is how fucking angry I am with her. She did this for me? Did she ever consider how fucking destroyed I'd be without her? She's more dangerous than Psycho and I put together, because even we wouldn't have done this. What the fuck was she thinking?

"Hold it together, brother," Bones says, as if he can read my mind, as if he knows I'm thinking that last night was the last time I would ever hold her.

"Everybody out except Reaper. I need a minute with my brother. We'll meet you outside. Give us ten minutes."

Everybody files out of the room, and he rises from his desk and sits beside me on the couch.

"Alright, brother, it's just us now. You have ten minutes to fall apart, and then you'll get your shit together, so we can do what we need to do to get your girl back to you."

I shake my head and then put my face in my hands.

"She's probably already dead, Bones. You know the way he is. Either that, or right now she's wishing she was."

He places his hand on my shoulder.

"We aren't going to think about that right now because, yes, any other woman would be dead, but your girl just might be crazy enough to survive until we get there."

I glance over to him and admit, "I'm so fucking in love with her, and I don't think I'll survive losing her."

He grins. "I knew that already, Reaper. I saw the way you looked at her, so I knew, before I asked you how serious it was, what your answer would be."

"She's everything," I say under my breath.

"Yeah, I know. A couple that slays together, stays together, and all that."

I chuckle, and he sighs audibly.

"The other De Lucas should be here, so let's go do your favorite thing in the world."

Rising off the couch, I follow him and say, "I think it's my second favorite thing now."

He turns to me with a shocked expression.

"That must be one magical fucking pussy."

Chapter Forty-Four

BELLA

Reaching under my skirt, I pull my knife out and hold it for him to see, and he smirks at me.

"Oh, that's cute. You brought a knife to a, well, *pipe fight*."

He chuckles like he's funny and he's not. There is no fucking way he's doing to me what he did to Nico.

Stepping closer to me, he grins. "This is beautiful, you know that?"

Rolling my eyes, I take two steps back. "What is?"

His grin widens to a creepy point, like the *Joker*. "When my nephew finds you, it's going to destroy him. You see, I've been waiting for a way to hurt him after what he did to me. Payback's a bitch, and this one, I'm sure, is going to hurt like a motherfucker."

He can't possibly know much about Nico and I, because even his brothers don't know a lot. Or at least Bones didn't seem to. Frank comes closer, and I swing my leg up to kick him, but he grabs it, twists, and brings me to the floor. I land with a thud on my stomach, and he hits me in the back with the pipe. I scream in pain but fight through it, and turn myself over and get to my feet. His eyes darken, as he growls like an angry animal.

"You're mine, fucking whore. I'll fuck you. And then I'll kill you."

The knife is still clenched in my hand and, as he charges at me again, I swipe it down his arm. It's not a deep cut, but it's enough to make him grimace from the sting. Again he swings the pipe and hits my arm, causing a blood-curdling cry to escape from my lungs, and I think my arm is broken, but I won't stop because if I do, I'm dead.

"Are you prepared to die for your cause?"

I stare at him in the eyes as I hold my ground.

"Yes. One of us will die. And it's going to be you."

He stops moving and laughs dramatically, throwing his head back, and I take the only opportunity I might have.

I plunge the knife into his stomach, and his eyes widen, as he grabs my hair and brings me to the floor.

Frank kneels on my back, pushing down with what feels like all of his strength, I try to throw him off me, but I can't. He's got to be at least two hundred pounds, and I can barely breathe, let alone move.

"I like this. Skirts mean easy access, sweetheart."

The tears pour from my eyes, as I mourn for the love of my life, and the pain I know he's going to be subjected to. The guilt consumes me, because I did this. I bit off more than I can chew, and he's going to be the one that has to live with my decisions.

I tried, Nico.

With one hand, he lifts my skirt and tears my panties from my body, and suddenly stops and chuckles when he sees Nico's name on my ass.

"Ahhh, well, look at this. It would appear to me that my nephew is more like me than his father. Let me guess, you didn't have a say in this, did you? This is some sick twisted shit. I'm so proud, I could cry."

He inserts the lead pipe into my pussy, and I scream while he laughs. The pain is excruciating, and feels like I'm being ripped in two.

I cry out for everything I feel. The physical pain. The violation. The fact that Nico will never forgive me. I did this, and I have no one to blame. Reaching under my skirt, I grab the other knife and swing my arm back, and stab him. He lands on top of me, and I still can't move. I struggle to move him off me, and eventually his body shifts to the floor with a thud, but as I try to retrieve the pipe, the dizziness sets in and I see stars, followed by pitch black.

Chapter Forty-Five
REAPER

We all pile into the armored van and head toward Frank's house. I've known where he was my entire life. There has never been a time when I didn't. When I told her to let it go, because the only reason I hadn't killed him is because I couldn't stand to be in presence long enough to do it, I was being honest. Even my brothers were surprised he wasn't already dead, after what he did to me. And I suppose I understand that, because normally he would've been, but they also don't understand what that does to a man. How it affects his thought process. I'm not okay, I haven't been for a long time, but the damage is done. I probably would've turned into a killer regardless, after all, my first kill was when I was a little kid. Would I have become the man I am now? I'll never know, because I wasn't ever given the chance to find out. I think it's why I formed such a close bond with Athena, because she understands what it's like. Even though I never told her what happened to me, somehow she knew something had happened to me. She never bought that I was just the way I was, as Bones suggested.

My brothers are all dressed in black pants and dress shirts, like they're going to a fucking business meeting, as are the De Luca brothers. I'm the only one in jeans and a t-shirt. All of us wear matching holsters and guns. We have more weapons on us than the military. Okay, maybe not that much, but pretty fucking close. Our intel tells us Frank has a total of forty guards scattered on the grounds, all of them Abruzzo men. I asked Bones why they would protect him to this degree, and he said he has something they want. Probably information on our family. Obviously, information he intends to use, to wipe us out.

Damian De Luca is driving, while the rest of us are in the back of the van. There's a lot of us and it's a tight fucking fit.

Bones instructs us as to how he wants things handled.

"The De Lucas will take the east side of the yard. We'll take the west. Then we'll meet in the back, and clear everything there as quietly as possible, before we breach the house. If he knows we're there, he will probably kill her."

Psycho nudges me in the shoulder.

"You alright, man?"

I shake my head no and add, "I'll hold it together until she's safe, and then I might kill everybody in the fucking state."

The fact that I don't even know if she'll be alive when we get there, has me ready to jump out of my skin, and being so fucking angry with her has me pissed off at myself, because somehow I know we aren't going to find her unscathed. Nobody goes up against Frank Bonetti, and walks away uninjured. It's not how it works. The only reason my father became the powerful man he was, is because he was the first-born male. Had my grandfather made choices like my dad did, it would've been a different outcome.

"Hey, Killer," Kage says and I roll my eyes. He calls me that when he's joking around, because he thinks its funny to call me a name one might call a rabid fucking dog. Although, it's better than what he called me when I was a kid; Emo.

"What?" I grunt, letting him know I'm irritated.

He tilts his head to the side. "Reaper, sorry. I just wanted to say, you got this. Everything is going to turn out fine. You'll marry your girl and have a dozen serial killer babies."

Bones snorts. "Kage, shut up. Don't put fucking ideas in his head."

Emotions have never been our strong suit. As I've grown, I bury mine and refuse to show them, mostly. Kage makes jokes, because he also cannot handle them. Bones is a bit of a mix. And Psycho, I'm pretty sure he doesn't even have any feelings. While I don't show it a lot, I'm the one that feels the most. And I know that's why they are all worried about me, given the situation. I've never had a girlfriend, and they've figured out that Bella is everything to me.

"If you see cameras, disable them," Bones says, as we reach our stopping point. If we pull up to the house in an armored vehicle, we'll have a lot of guards on us very quickly. It's much easier if we can take them a couple at a time. If we're surrounded by forty at once, we will have casualties.

We get out of the van, and Bones asks quietly, "Everybody clear on how we're approaching this?"

As a collective unit we nod, and my brother turns to me. "I want you close to me."

I would like to argue with him, because I don't want to be treated like a kid, when I'm a grown man, but I ignore it because that's not what's important.

From a distance, Drake De Luca raises his weapon as we approach, shoots the guard at the gate square in the eye, and whispers, 'boo-yah'.

I roll my eyes as we separate to our areas. We take the west, and notice there are small groups of guards in several different directions, smoking and talking amongst themselves, like they're on break. I'm guessing they're not, because, wouldn't breaks be a group at a time? Do they even get breaks? Who knows. Myself and my brothers all raise our weapons, and Bones and I take out the first group. We are using silencers, but there's still noise when we fire, and the second group turns around as Kage and Psycho take them out.

As we walk further, Psycho complains in a whisper.

"Guns are fucking boring. A knife would be more fun."

I can't help but smile, as I think of how much my girl will get along with at least one of my brothers.

Please be alive.

We approach three more groups, and take them out with minimal sound, to not alert the other guards. Stepping over the dead bodies, we round the corner when one nobody saw comes out, and smacks me across the face with his gun. Kage points his gun at his head and shoots.

Once we make it to the back, we're all surprised, when we meet up with the De Lucas, that there are no guards at the back.

"Be ready. There could be more inside the house," Bones says. We walk back around to the front door, and again are surprised that it's unlocked.

We get through the entry-way, and not making noise is no longer an option. Our footwear taps against the tile, announcing our presence, but then it doesn't matter.

Bones says, "She's right here."

He looks back at me, and I know by the look on his face, we're too late.

My brother turns to everyone else.

"Turn around. He doesn't need you looking."

All the air escapes from my lungs as I stare at her unmoving body, with a fucking lead pipe protruding from her pussy. As much as I want to look away, I can't tear my eyes from her. My gaze moves from the ripped shirt she's wearing, her torn panties on the floor beside her, her bloody hands, and the puddle of blood around her. The big blue bruise on her cheek causes a fire to grow in my blood. A homicidal rage fills me, one I can't do anything about because Frank is already dead. The anger and heartbreak fight for dominance, and the latter wins out. The crushing pain in my chest is far more intense than when there was a knife plunged inside it.

I go to grab the pipe and Bones yells, "Leave it. If you remove it, it could cause more damage than leaving it. Check for a pulse."

Kneeling beside her head, I stroke her hair, my beautiful Bella.

"Baby. Please be okay, I need you with me."

Leaning down, I kiss her cheek.

"You did good, baby. You killed him, didn't you?"

Pressing my hand to her neck, I breathe a sigh of relief when I feel her pulse.

"She's alive," I cry in a voice I don't recognize.

"Pick her up carefully, and I'll call the family doctor and let him know we're on our way."

I pull her skirt down, and lift her into my arms and tell Bones, "Nobody fucking looks at this."

He shakes his head. "I promise you. They will all act with the respect this situation deserves."

I already know Bella would be devastated to know these men saw this. Especially my brothers.

Carrying her through the house, I step over the dead bodies as I walk to the van, talking to her the entire time.

"You're in a lot of trouble, you know that, right?"

I slide into the back of the van, and Bones hands me a blanket so I can cover her legs, and he says the De Lucas will catch another ride to give us privacy. My brothers get into the back while Bones gets into the driver's seat and he quickly takes off.

Both Kage and Psycho are careful not to look at her, but they talk to me.

Kage says, "I'm glad she's alive, man. She can heal from other shit, she'll be okay."

Instantly the rage fills me, because he's referring to the fucking lead pipe in her pussy. I almost wish she hadn't killed him, so I could.

They are quiet for a few minutes, and Kage says, "I got a girl in a cage. If you want to kill her, you can."

I shake my head at him.

"Why do you have a girl in a cage?"

He shrugs. "Why do you kill people?"

Valid fucking point.

I look down at Bella, as she moans in my arms.

"Ow," she cries.

"I'm here, living dead girl. I know it hurts, but you'll be okay."

She doesn't open her eyes, but tears slip down her cheeks as she whispers my name.

Chapter Forty-Six
REAPER

I follow Bones inside with Bella in my arms, pulled against my chest, and Athena looks on with a face that reflects horror as I follow Bones upstairs. We go into a guest bedroom, and I lay her on the bed.

"I'm gonna give you two privacy, but if you need anything, yell for me. The doctor is on his way. You should stay here for a few days. Athena will probably be good for her."

I know what he's referring to, but I don't respond. That will ultimately be up to Bella. Her lashes flutter open, and she quickly turns her head away from me.

I stroke her hair while she speaks low, but above a whisper.

"Don't touch me. Please get your hands off me."

Immediately, I remove my hands from her and try to reassure her, "Baby, it's Nico."

Through a clenched jaw, she says, "I know who you are. Don't fucking touch me."

I don't have very long to contemplate what's going on, before there's a knock at the bedroom door, and the doctor comes in.

He nods to me.

"Dr. Messina. Bones asked me to help. He informed me of the situation."

Walking over to Bella, he introduces himself.

"Can Reaper stay in the room? Or would you rather he leave?"

She sobs loudly, and it tears me to shreds.

"Please make him leave."

I could easily tell the doctor to fuck off and refuse to leave, but if this is what she wants, I should go. Standing in the hallway, Athena comes up to me, with a look of concern on her face. She wraps her arms around me as Bones looks on. Normally, my brother would tell me to get my hands off his wife, but he doesn't.

"She asked me to leave."

Athena takes my hand and pulls me to the sitting room, the next room over. "I want to talk to you about something."

We walk in and she points to the couch. "Sit."

Bones stands in the doorway, staring at my sister-in-law like she hung the goddamn moon, and for the first time I get it. She sits beside me.

"Reaper, what she went through, nobody other than her even knows how bad it was, but we know enough to know she's likely traumatized. After you guys found me, I felt ashamed, scared, and thought Luca would look at me differently. He showed me love and patience, and eventually I found myself on the other side of things, but it wasn't an immediate process. The only way out of this is through. She has to go through it, and so do you."

"Did you tell Bones not to touch you? And to leave?"

She shakes her head no and places her hand over mine.

"Everybody's experience is different. How she processes things will not necessarily be the same as it was for me. Patience is the only way. Give her what she needs. If you don't know what that is, ask her."

I shake my head.

"She's going to leave me, and I'm going to let her."

"What?" Bones says, as he walks over to us and sits on the chair beside the couch.

"We did not just go through this for you to not be with her."

Athena holds up her hand. "Luca. Not now."

"Talk to me. What makes you say that?"

I look away from my sister-in-law, because right now I can't handle her kind eyes, the way she looks at me like I'm something other than what I am.

Hanging my head down, I admit, "This is my fault. Everything that happened to her is because of me."

I jump when I hear her screaming, and immediately go to knock the fucking doctor on his ass, but Bones stops me.

"Let him do his job."

"Can I have a few minutes alone with Reaper?"

He growls, "No."

She tilts her head at him. "Luca."

With a glare, he says, "Butterfly."

Athena does not back down from him, she persists, "Luca. Go check on your brothers. I want to talk to Reaper alone."

He walks to the door and turns to me with a glare. "Keep your fucking hands off my wife."

"There you are. I thought we lost you."

Bones grumbles something inaudible as he walks out the door.

"There are no annoying men here now, to tell you not to feel or express emotion. Talk to me."

I sigh and close my eyes, so I don't have to look at her facial expressions.

"Short version is my uncle raped me when I was a kid, for years, with a pipe. I told Bella because, I don't know, I had some stupid idea that she had to know me completely, and why I'm so fucked up. Also, I told her I hadn't killed him, because I couldn't stand to be in the room with him long enough, so crazy thing that she is, she did it herself. If I had the balls to do it, this never would have happened. If I did the right thing, she wouldn't be in there with…"

I don't finish my sentence, because I can't even fucking say it.

"The point is, this is my fault. I did this. I am the reason she ever killed anyone. This is all my doing."

"I killed my father for what he did to me."

Glancing up at her, I'm confused, because I was there.

"I could've never done that without my husband, and his brothers there. Would I have ever gone back to face him on my own? Not a

209

chance. Because that is trauma, Reaper. The fear of facing him does not make you weak. When you're put through something like that, you don't want to go face the monster who hurt you."

I don't respond, because I'm not sure how to, and she continues.

"This is not your fault. It's not hers either. There's one person to blame for this, and according to Luca, he's dead. Give her time. Be there for her, and you'll both get through this. Show her how much you love her, and that this changed nothing, because I wouldn't be surprised to find out that's what she fears most."

The doctor knocks on the door and enters, ending our conversation.

He points to Luca's vacated chair.

"May I?"

I nod, and he takes a seat.

"Physically, she's going to be okay. The pipe didn't appear to cause any damage, but she's going to need some further testing to be sure. However, I didn't see any tearing, or anything that I would be immediately concerned about."

Dragging my hand down my face, I say, "She was unconscious when we found her. Is that a concern?"

His phone buzzes, but he silences it and responds, "Not really. It's possible she passed out from the trauma, or the pain. I guarantee it wasn't pleasant. I did check her head for wounds, and I didn't see anything obvious. Also, she said she didn't hit her head. Her memory is intact, and she was able to recount details of the event."

He pushes the glasses back on his face.

"I asked her if she would be willing to speak with a therapist, and she declined. Ultimately, that has to be her decision, but it is something I'd recommend. Bones and Athena can tell you, we have a few that work with mafia families. They're familiar with your lives."

He means crime, and that they won't run to the police with information.

"That's not why she said no. I don't know why she won't see someone, but Bella doesn't come from the crime world. She wouldn't know about the risks involved with speaking to the wrong people."

He hands me a card.

"If she needs anything, call me. I'm available for your family twenty-four/seven. And if she changes her mind, let me know."

Chapter Forty-Seven
BELLA

There's a knock at the door, and I yell, "Go away, Nico."

A feminine voice responds, "It's Athena. He isn't with me. Can I come in?"

I can't really tell her no, since I'm guessing this is her house. I know it isn't Nico's.

"Sure."

She comes in and closes the door behind her, and sits on the chair beside the bed.

"I just wanted to talk if that's okay."

Pulling the blankets over my legs, I sit up slightly. "That's fine."

"I've been where you are. I'll spare you the details, but my father did terrible things to me. And I know you've been through so much, but I'm here to tell you there's healing. It's not always going to be like it is right now."

I look down at the blanket, and rub my finger across the blue material.

"He must hate me. I can't even look at him, because I'm so ashamed. I did this. Without telling him, I walked into his uncle's house thinking I could handle it, and look what happened."

She smiles at me.

"And you killed him. Fucking badass."

I shrug my shoulders.

"And got myself raped."

She rubs her belly as she shakes her head.

"That doesn't take away what you did. How many women have the guts to go into a home, guarded by men with guns, to avenge what has been done to the man they love? Not many. In my book, you're a badass. You knew going in there that you might not come out alive, didn't you? You had to have. And yet, Reaper was worth it to you."

"He's worth everything," I whisper.

Folding her hands over her stomach, she says, "That man is broken right now. He loves you in the same way his brother loves me. And he's terrified he's going to lose you, because he has convinced himself this is his fault. I know you know Reaper well, and I'm not suggesting otherwise, but I want to tell you what I know about him. He has killed far more people than any of his brothers, but as we all now know he has also endured more. Reaper has a big heart that feels deeply. Once I got to know him, I told my husband if he ever fell in love, it would be permanent, because that's the man he is. He's complex. Reaper will take a life without batting an eye, but those he loves, he loves fiercely. Yet if you ask him to let you go, he will, because he thinks he did this to you, and we both know he didn't. I really hope you don't ask him to do that, because honestly, I'm not sure he'd ever recover from losing you. I'm not trying to make you feel guilty. I just want you to know what's at stake before you see him."

Glancing up at her, I say, "It seems you two are close."

She nods. "When I came into this family, I had no one. Literally no one. One day I'll tell you the story. All three of them welcomed me with open arms, but Reaper is different from the other two. There was something in him I recognized. I think I sensed the trauma, and he quickly became one of my favorite people in the world."

She rises from the chair with a bit of trouble.

"I have to use the restroom. You have no idea how much a pregnant woman pees. Thank you for listening. You can say no, but can he come in? He just wants to be in the same room as you."

"Yeah, he can come in."

Smiling softly, she says, "I'll check on you later."

A few minutes after she leaves, he comes in, and I still have trouble looking at him. His face is long, his head down as if he's ashamed. He probably is. Of me. Finding me the way he did, how do you ever get that image out of your mind?

He takes a seat in the chair and, even without looking at him, I can feel his eyes on me. The burn is uncomfortable, like he's a stranger.

"Bella, I'm sorry. You're right to be angry with me. I probably can't ever make this up to you. I love you, and I'll never fucking forgive myself for this."

His words confuse the hell out of me. Why would I be angry with him for something I did? It was my choices that led to everything that happened.

"This wasn't your fault, Nico. I'm the one who caused what he did."

Shaking his head, he says, "I should've killed him a long time ago, and if I had, you wouldn't have felt the need to put yourself in danger."

"Again, it wasn't your fault, but I know this changes things, so I'm going to take a shower, if your brother wouldn't mind too much, and I'll be on my way."

Chapter Forty-Eight
Reaper

I say nothing as she gets up and goes into the bathroom. My mind is fucking racing, and my heart pounds with defeat. The desire to lock her up and keep her with me is strong. So fucking strong, but I can't. After what she's been through, I can't do it. So much has happened between us, and I can't bring myself to cause her more pain, even if losing her will destroy me. This is the problem with being given something so incredible. I was fine before, but suddenly, the devastation is as all-consuming as she is.

When she comes back into the bedroom, she's wearing a t-shirt and yoga pants. Athena must have left them for her. She looks stunning as usual, with freshly cleaned skin and wet hair. I just want to fucking hold her in my arms, but I know I can't.

This fucking hurts.

"It changes nothing for me. My feelings for you have never wavered. Go ahead and leave me, living dead girl. Take the fucking breath from my lungs. Yank out the heart from my chest. Just know, I'll never be far. I'll be watching, because I have no other choice. The only way you'll truly be rid of me is to kill me, and I hope you do. I won't even fight you."

She sits on the bed and sighs audibly.

"How can you ever look at me, and not see what you saw?"

Clenching my fists, I say, "When I look at you, I see you. Like I always have. My hands are in fists so I can stop myself from touching you, when my fingers and arms physically ache to hold you. Not so long ago, you told me not to push you away. And yet you're doing the same thing right now. I deserve to lose you, but I still can't bear it. Will I ever forget what he did to you? No. When I look at you, I don't see that. I see my beautiful girl that I don't know how to fucking live without."

"Nico," she whispers, as a tear rolls down her cheek.

"I don't know how to do this. The only thing I know how to do is run from shit."

Fuck this. I cannot handle this distance. Rising from the chair, I go over to the bed and sit beside her, and pull her into my arms. She punches me in the chest repeatedly, but I don't let her go. Instead, I lift her and move to the head of the bed, and lay down, holding her tight. She sobs into my chest, but I don't release her.

"I'm sorry. I can't do the right thing."

Sighing, I continue, "I told myself if you wanted me to let you go, I would, but I can't. For you, I desperately want to be a better man than I am, but I can't be"

She clutches onto my shirt, like she's holding on for dear life. And I inhale the scent of her hair and instantly don't like it. She doesn't smell like she usually does, because the shampoo is different.

"Before I passed out, I was cursing myself, because I knew you wouldn't forgive me for letting another man touch me like that."

I kiss the top of her head, because I can't stop myself.

"You didn't let him. Did you ask him to do that to you? I bet not. You didn't let him, any more than I let him, baby."

She pulls her head back and looks me in the eyes, for the first time since I found her.

"I'm sorry he hurt you. It was stupid, I know that now, but I wanted to make him pay for what he did to you."

Placing my palm on the side of her face, I shake my head.

"It wasn't stupid. It was dangerous, yet beautiful. Nobody has ever stood up for me like that. Do I wish you hadn't done that? Yes, but don't think it doesn't mean anything, because it means a lot. And you fucking killed him. Not without injuries, but you did make him pay."

She slides her hand inside my shirt, and holds it against my heart.

Sighing in contentment, I ask her the one question that needs to be answered.

"Are you using drugs?"

Her glare is instant and beautiful, but I still want to know.

"The doctor gave me something for the pain. I'm not *using* drugs."

"I'm referring to you arranging to buy drugs prior to going to the house."

Bella's mouth forms the perfect 'O' as realization dawns on her.

"I was hoping to sneak up on him, and take him out easily. How did you know?"

Smirking at her, I say, "Every keystroke on my laptop is recorded. Also, you bought drugs from my family, just so you know."

Her eyelids get heavy, and I pull her head back to my chest.

"Sleep, baby."

Almost instantly, she relaxes and slumbers in my arms, exactly where she's supposed to be. I stare at her face, while she gets the rest she needs, and can't believe I thought for a second I could let her go. I'll help her release her rage. If I have to line up dozens of people for her to kill, I will. She can squeeze the breath from their lungs, or gut them like a fish. Whatever she needs, she will have.

"Nico," she gasps, as she claws at the skin covering my heart.

"It's okay, baby, I'm right here."

Relaxing her hands, she whispers, "I thought-"

Kissing her on the top of her head, I reassure her, or at least try.

"I'm right here, and I'm not going anywhere. If I have to fucking piss, I'm taking you with me."

She sighs with contentment, and, fuck does that sound good. I hold her tighter, while my chest squeezes.

I keep my gaze on her, and can't stop thinking about how I could've lost her, permanently. I'll never fucking allow that again.

Chapter Forty-Nine
BELLA

I wake to Nico holding onto me like I might disappear if he relaxes his hold. When I open my eyes, he's staring into them, and wiping tears from my face.

"Was I crying?"

He nods and leans down, kissing my cheek.

"I don't remember. Fuck. I hate this. I need-"

"What do you need, baby?"

I sigh loudly.

"Violence. I need violence, Nico."

He watches me cautiously.

"Are you sure it's not too soon?"

Raising an eyebrow, I ask, "Nico Bonetti, have you gone soft?"

His lips turn up into that delicious smirk that I love so much.

"For you? Softer than one of those fucking memory foam pillows. For the rest of the world? Not a fucking chance. You want to go kill people, living dead girl?"

I nod with a sigh. "I really do."

As I sit up, he places his hands on either side of my face, and stares into my eyes.

"My savage little angel of death."

His gaze drops to my lips, and he closes his eyes like he's trying to control himself.

"I'm not going to, but fuck, baby, I miss you and I want to kiss you, so badly it hurts."

"Kiss me, Nico," I whisper.

He pops his eyes open. "Are you sure?"

I thread my fingers into the back of his hair, and pull his head closer to me.

"I don't know that I'm ready for more yet, but yes, Nico, I'm sure. Fucking kiss me."

Closing the gap between us, he swipes his tongue against my closed lips, and groans my name softly.

Sliding his hands from my face to my hair, he tangles his fingers in my strands and presses his lips to mine in a slow kiss. He slides his tongue against mine, and I moan into his mouth as he tilts my head to the side, as if he needs more. Even when I thought Nico was a monster, he always lit me on fire. From day one, there's been this visceral connection between us, even when I wanted to deny it.

Pulling my hair, he forces my head back, and presses his mouth to my throat.

"Just kissing, nothing more," he murmurs against my skin, as he alternates between licks, bites, and soft kisses with his lips.

"Nico," I whimper.

If I said I didn't want him, it'd be a lie, but I think it's too soon. I'm afraid of how I'll react, so we need to wait.

Sliding his arms around my back, he pulls me close to him, as he buries his face in the crook of my neck, and speaks low against my skin.

"Thank you. Jesus Christ. Thank you, baby."

Climbing onto my knees, I kiss his neck.

"Thank you for being understanding."

He chuckles softly.

"Are you ready to depopulate the earth?"

I pull back and smile at him.

"Let's start at Walmart. I feel like there are way too many people there."

He laughs as he pulls me off the bed.

"Fucking savage, living dead girl."

He takes my hand and walks me downstairs, and I immediately feel embarrassed when I spot not only Athena and Bones, but his other brothers.

"Psycho, give me your knife."

He arches his eyebrow and glares at him.

"Why?"

Nico holds his hand out to him, and says, "We're going out, so living dead girl can let out some rage. She might want to make people bleed."

Bones groans, as he holds his pregnant wife on his lap.

"Jesus Christ. This family is going to hell."

Psycho lifts his gaze, and tilts his head at me with a questioning expression.

"You cut people, princess?"

I shrug. "I have. Only once, but I liked it. Blood makes it better."

"A girl after my own heart. How'd you end up with the silent killer here?"

Nico clutches my hand with his free one and growls.

"Give me the knife, and get your fucking eyes off my girl, dickhead."

He chuckles in response and hands him the weapon, and Nico spins me around to leave.

Chapter Fifty
REAPER

There is a pretty good chance my girl is more unhinged than I am, which surprises me, but does not disappoint me. I watch her, as she holds a blonde woman with her head hanging over what will become her grave, in my family's cemetery, so that we don't have blood all over the place, which will only result in a bitch-fest from my brother. And he wouldn't be wrong. Just because we can deal with issues, doesn't mean we should create them. It's much easier to prevent the problems we can. I love watching her kill. It's a beautiful sight. Especially when they cry and beg for their life. She isn't cruel, she's gentle as she ushers them into the afterlife. Soothing.

Bella speaks in a low, even tone to the woman.

"Shhhh. It's almost over."

She sits on top of her, straddling her chest with her arms underneath her, as she takes my brother's knife and cuts her throat. Blood pours from her body as Bella rolls her into the grave. I've never had an affinity for blood. Psycho does, I don't, although I'm not afraid of it either. I have a fear of few things. Yet, when she rises and turns to me, with the bloody knife in her grasp, and a little blood on her hand, I'm hard as a rock. She's stunning with murderous wide eyes, a smear of blood on her cheek, and a deadly expression.

I hold out the towel to wrap the knife in, as she walks over to me with a heated expression that has me ready to lose my mind.

"Take your clothes off, Nico," she says as she takes the towel from me, wrapping the knife in it, before placing it on the ground.

"What?"

Narrowing her gaze at me, she repeats herself, "Take your clothes off."

"Bella," I warn.

"Are you going to give me what I need or not?"

I step closer to her, lower my head, and stare into her eyes.

"If you're sure you're ready."

She shakes her head.

"I don't know that I am, but I need you to silence his voice. I want to forget, even if it's only for a few minutes. So please give me what I need most. *You.* Take your shirt off, pull your pants down and lie on the ground."

She watches me as I pull my shirt over my head, and then she removes the t-shirt and yoga pants that Athena left for her, along with shoes that must also be my sister-in-law's.

I pull my jeans down and lie on the cold, hard ground, and she quickly removes her bra and comes over to me.

"Hands down until I tell you it's okay."

I place my hands, palms down, on the grass as she climbs over me, and straddles my lap. Bella moves her wet pussy up and down my hard cock, and I groan because she feels so fucking good, but I'm dying to touch her.

Lifting her ass up, she takes me into her hand and pushes me inside her pussy, with a sweet little whimper. She sinks down on me, taking all of me in, and leans over me, placing her hands on my arms, as she presses her lips to mine. At first, I think it's going to be sweet, but it turns into a ravenous one, as she lifts herself on and off of me.

"This isn't working," she complains.

"What do you need, Bella?"

Lifting herself off my chest, she says, "You. Like we always are. Fuck me. Touch me. Remind me that I'm yours. Control me."

Carefully, I turn us over so she's laying on the ground. I place one hand beside her head, to hold myself up slightly, and cup her tit with my other hand before pinching her nipple.

"Nico," she gasps.

Wrapping her arms around my back, and legs around my ass, she pulls me down on top of her.

"Give me your weight, Nico. Everything."

I bury my face in the side of her neck, and inhale the scent I love so fucking much, as I drive into her over and over again.

"You don't need a reminder that you're mine, baby. You have been, since the moment I looked into your beautiful eyes. And you will be even at your death."

I make sure I hit her clit with my pelvis on every thrust, and she begins to fall apart. Lifting myself so I can watch her face, I think I fall in love with her all over again.

"That's my girl. Come for me."

"Nico!" she screams as her pussy chokes my cock, and tries to keep it inside her.

I stare at her, as her eyes roll back into her head, and she trembles for me, with a scream that's only for me.

"Good girl. You see, I own you. Your orgasms, your sounds, your heart, your entire fucking body. This is mine, and you'll never need a reminder, but I'm happy to give you one, anyway."

She whimpers and then speaks low.

"Nico, take me to the brink of death and bring me back to life, like only you can."

Wrapping my hand around her throat, I growl, "Die for me, and then live for me."

"Always," she gasps, seconds before I take away her breath, and fuck her harder.

When I let go, she gasps and trembles from her powerful orgasm, and takes me with her. I come inside her and groan, "I can't wait for your belly to swell with our baby."

"Nico, I can't get pregnant."

My heart fucking drops, because I was worried about this after what happened.

She holds her hand to my face.

"No, you don't understand. I can't get pregnant right now, because I'm already pregnant. The doctor was surprised I didn't miscarry. Our little baby is tucked safely in there."

I stare at her, completely stunned.

"You're pregnant. I'm going to be a father?"

She smiles that smile that makes my heart beat faster.

"I'm pregnant, Nico."

Getting onto my knees, I stare at her beautiful body, and place my hand on her stomach.

"A family of my own? Everybody thought it wasn't possible because I'm crazy."

Bella sits up and wraps her arms around my neck.

"You just needed to let someone see you, Nico. I see you and I love you. My insanity matches yours. I'd kill a million people just to hear your voice again if I ever lost you."

Taking her face in my hands, I say, "If you die before me, I'll throw myself in the grave with you, because life without you is not worth living."

I kiss her softly and then pull back with a grin.

"Hey, crazy girl, are you ready to go tell my family?"

She flashes me a shocked expression.

"Don't you want to wait until I'm further along?"

"Nope. I'm going to rent a fucking neon sign."

We pull apart and start getting dressed, and I think out loud.

"Kage says we should have twelve babies, and I think he's right."

She gasps loudly. "I'm going to kill your brother."

"Maybe a few ground rules," I say with an arched brow.

"Kill who you want, baby, but not my family."

"Fine," she says as she pulls her pants on.

I wrap my arms around her, and she once again rocks my world.

"Thank you. You did indeed break me, Nico, but then you put me back together, as a better version of myself."

Do I regret all the things I did to her in the beginning? Not a fucking chance, because it got us to where we are now. I don't know if I'm actually crazy, but as long as I've got my living dead girl, I really don't fucking care.

THE END

Keep reading for the epilogue(s)!

Epilogue One

Bones runs his hand through his hair, and I chuckle, because he really reminds me of our dad when he does that.

"You're sure she's pregnant?"

I'm slightly thrown off by his question.

"Yeah. The doctor did a test and said she was."

"Congratulations, Reaper. Wow. That's a lot to take in."

I sit in the seat across from his desk and shake my head.

"I'm happy. Can you not be fucking happy for me?"

Bones folds his hands over his desk and sighs.

"I'm happy for you, Nico. I am. I just worry about you. How does a baby fit into your life of homicide?"

I shrug. "I don't know. People get date nights, right?"

He looks to the ceiling like it'll help him.

"Okay, maybe we still do it, but slow down a little."

"Or you kill people I tell you to. We've got the Abruzzos to deal with still."

I hold my hands up. "No guarantees, but I'll try, alright? But you've got to let my girl in on it."

He shakes his head no.

"There's no fucking way she's coming with us to kill those fucking assholes. It's dangerous, and if she's carrying my niece or nephew, not a chance."

"Uncle Bones. Sounds good, doesn't it?"

He chuckles, and then his face gets serious again.

"I know you've always felt like the odd brother that doesn't fit with the rest of us, but you do. We all kill, you aren't that different, you just literally seek it out. None of us think you're a monster. As I lead this family, it's part of my job to minimize the problems, so I need you to maybe think a little more about who can see you, and who the person is. Maybe stay away from rival families, until you're told to go after them."

I nod. "Yeah, that was reckless, and could've ended badly for Bella."

Hell, it did end badly, but it could've been worse.

"Look at you, *Papa*. Already growing up," he says with a smirk, but then his face turns serious.

"We need to beef up the men on your property. You've got Bella now, a baby on the way, and working for the family will attract enemy attention. They're unlikely to go after you, Reaper. Your woman and child will be the target, so let's protect them."

I nod in agreement, because I know this to be true, and I'll do anything to prevent them from being hurt.

He reaches out his hand and I shake it.

"Welcome back, brother, where you belong."

"Thank you, Bones."

He shakes his head as he sits back and takes a sip of his drink.

"For what it's worth, our father didn't handle things appropriately with your situation, and he did far more damage with how he approached things. You were a casualty of that choice. Had we known, we would've killed that fucker a long time ago. Family or not. And instead of using your gifts, he cast you out. I'll never agree with that decision."

Bones rises from his chair and nods to the door.

"Let's get back to the others. I've reached the limit on how long I can be away from my butterfly."

There was a time I would've thought that was pathetic, but I get it now. After being away from Bella for too long, the edginess sets in, and I'm ready to jump out of my skin. If I can't touch her, she isn't fucking close enough. Some people might say it's an unhealthy obsession, but I think it's a perfect one.

We walk down the stairs together, and I have to swallow the lump in my throat as I watch her interacting with my family, as if she's known them forever. Psycho is showing her his special knife. He was fourteen, and made his first kill with his enemy's knife, and he took it and it's sort of a trophy for him. I watch her talk animatedly, as she regales my two brothers with all the details of her kill from earlier tonight. I love that Athena, who isn't really like us, listens attentively. That's probably my favorite thing about my brother's wife. She accepts you even if she doesn't necessarily agree with your choices. I can already tell that she and my Bella are going to be friends. Can a serial killer actually have a happy ending?

Fuck. It would appear so.

I can't imagine an asshole like me could get any happier than this.

Epilogue Two
BELLA

Nico comes running into the living room where I sit reading a book, and starts waving his hands in the air.

"It's time. We have to go. She's getting ready to push."

I giggle at the way he's panicking, and wonder what he'll be like when the time comes for our baby to be born.

Athena has been in labor for three days, so this isn't exactly a surprise. We knew at some point she would progress and give birth.

"Nico."

He stops and stares at me as I shake my head.

"It's going to be okay."

Grabbing my hand, he pulls me off the couch and races to the door.

"I know it is. It's just excitement. I'm going to be a fucking uncle, and I can't wait to teach the baby everything I know."

I laugh as he opens the door to the car and buckles me in. Ever since he found out I was pregnant, his possessive mode has increased ten-fold, and he insists on doing everything for me. He cooks every meal, as if I might die a brutal death from using the dangerous stove.

"How's Bones?" I ask as he begins to drive away from our house.

He chuckles as he makes a turn.

"A goddamn mess. It's been no picnic for Athena, obviously, but watching her in pain for three days has been difficult. You know how he is when it comes to her."

I giggle.

"As bad as you are with me."

He glances over at me with a smirk on his face.

"That's not entirely true. I like causing you pain, living dead girl. I just won't allow anyone else to hurt you."

Taking my hand in his, he pulls it to his mouth, and kisses the back.

"Mine to hurt. Mine to protect."

I glance at him with a serious expression.

"What's the rule, Nico?"

He chuckles low, and it only increases my need for him.

"If I make it wet, I make it come."

"Exactly."

As he pulls into the hospital parking lot, he groans softly.

"And I will, but first, I want to see the little Bonetti."

I whine, "Then stop turning me on."

With a smirk, he says, "I can't help it, baby. It's a gift."

As frustrating as his cocky comment is, he's right, it is. How I was his first, I'll never know, because this man is a walking aphrodisiac.

Like always, after he parks, he gets out and walks around and opens my door, before unbuckling my seatbelt.

He helps me out of the car, and stares at me while placing his hand on my face.

"I'm so glad you're here with me for this. You're making a great moment perfect."

"Nico," I gasp, and he places his arm around my back, pulls me against his chest, and growls in my ear.

"Would you behave? I can smell your arousal, and it's driving me fucking crazy."

Athena told me that I would want it all the time, around my fourth or fifth month of pregnancy, but I'm not there yet, and still I want him constantly. As far as behaving myself, when Nico is around, I have zero control over my arousal, so either he needs to do something about it, or deal with it.

He pulls me in close to his side as we walk into the hospital.

"Try not to attract attention. I promised Bones I wouldn't do anything stupid today."

His phone starts chiming with an alert, so he looks down as we step into the elevator, and with a big goofy grin, he says, "Little Bonetti is here."

"Boy or a girl?" I ask as the door slides closed.

He shrugs. "I don't know. Kage sent me a text, but didn't say."

Once the doors re-open, he takes my hand and we walk to Athena's room. Walking in, I see something I never would've imagined. We are quiet, so we don't interrupt the moment between father and son.

Bones stares down at his newborn son, judging by the blue blanket, and I've never seen his face like this. Not stern, loving, yet so emotional.

"Atlas Bonetti, you have done the impossible. You made me a father. Something I never aspired to be, but now that you're here, it's everything I want. I'm in trouble though, son. I can already tell you're just like your mother and you, too, are going to change everything for me. I love you, son," Bones says to his little boy, as Athena looks on with tears streaming down her face. He looks over to Nico and says, "Come here. I'll introduce you to your nephew."

I go over to Athena and sit by her on the bed, and ask her how she's feeling.

She smiles softly.

"I'm so in love."

Nodding to Nico, she says, "Look."

Turning my head, I gaze at him holding his brand new nephew, as he talks to him in a quiet voice, and the baby has his hand wrapped around his finger.

"Hi. I'm your Uncle Reaper. One day it'll make sense, I promise. And just so you know, you have two other uncles, but I'm going to be your favorite."

The other two walk into the room and Psycho snorts loudly.

"Not a fucking chance."

Athena scowls at them both.

"Watch your language around him."

When they nod instead telling her off, I can't help but giggle, because I'm pretty sure if it were anybody else they would have.

She takes my hand in hers, and beams with pure happiness.

"You're next. Are you excited?"

"Yes," I say, but then admit, "And terrified."

I never had a great example of how to mother. My mom never had that bond with me that you hear almost every mom go on about. I think I was an inconvenience more than anything, yet also her way out of her own abusive upbringing. I was useful to her until I wasn't. And now I'm going to have a family of my own, and I'm terrified to make the same mistakes, but somehow I know we'll be better parents than mine were. Nico and I are not perfect people, in fact, we do things that most people in society would call heinous. Yet we both also have so much love for each other, and I know that will continue with our child.

Nico comes over with baby Atlas and asks, "Do you want to hold him?"

I glance over at Bones, who is standing in his normal stance, feet slightly spread and arms crossed, watching like a bomb is going to go off at any moment, and he'll have to rescue his wife and child. He's intense.

I shake my head no.

"It's okay. You hold him for me."

Nico arches a brow at me.

"Why don't you want to hold him?" he asks in a low voice.

I speak low back.

"Let's not make a big deal out of this, Nico. I don't want to make anyone uncomfortable."

He looks at Athena with a hurt expression.

"Can she not hold him?"

She laughs softly. "It's not me she's concerned about."

He looks at his brother. "Bones?"

Bones nods. "Go ahead. Hold your nephew."

I gasp, and as Nico places Atlas into my arms, my entire world shifts, because I feel something I've never felt before. *Acceptance.* By my family. We aren't all born into families that love us, and accept us for the weird people we are. Maybe we don't need to be, if we find the ones that take us with all our flaws.

Looking down at baby Atlas sleeping in my arms, I feel a sense of peace, of belonging, and somehow I know, I'm finally home.

KAGE'S BLURB IS ON THE NEXT PAGE!

BONETTI
BROTHERS

BOOK THREE

Rage

A DARK MAFIA ROMANCE

CHELLE ROSE

KAGE BLURB:

KAGE:

The instructions were clear. Go into the enemy compound and leave no one alive. My brother is the head of the family, and he makes the calls. Normally I go along with it, but not this time. I find Abruzzo's youngest daughter, a stunning redhead, cowering under a table, and decide she would look really pretty in my cage.

Raina looked so sweet and innocent, meek and mild. Much to my surprise, she's anything but. Playing with fire can get you burned, but somehow, I know it'll be worth it in the end. I live life dangerously, and there's nothing more threatening than her.

RAINA:

Killing most of my family was his first mistake. Taking me was his second. I'm not the little mouse he takes me for. Once he's in my trap, it won't just be him that pays the price for what he has done. His entire family will be gone. I'll light the match, and sit back and watch the show. And what a show it'll be.

All is fair in love and war. And this is war. Can Kage save his family, or is this the end of the Bonetti line?

ACKNOWLEDGEMENTS:

As always, thank you to my ARC, STREET and BETA teams. You guys rock.

Heather-
Thank you so much for beta reading Reaper and for encouraging me to write a book unlike anything I'd ever written.

Amazing Grace my PA-
Thank you for being you. You are amazing with everything you do. From graphics to keeping me on task to beta reading. Nothing goes unappreciated. Oh, and also for talking me off the ledge from time to time. Thank you for taking on my chaos.

To my Editor-
I'm so grateful for you. Thank you for helping me to not look like an idiot.

To my Cover Designer-
Thank you times a billion. I swear each cover you do is better than the one before. I appreciate your attention to detail on this cover, down to the creepy eyeballs on Reaper's shoulder.

To Ruth and Kendra-

You share nearly everything I post. Thank you. This means the world to me. You're both amazing and I hope you know how much I appreciate you.

To my Readers-

Thank you for taking a chance on my books. My goal is to take you on an entertaining ride that makes you feel something. I hope I've achieved that.

ALSO BY CHELLE ROSE:

Forbidden Desires Series

1. *Mercy www.books2read.com/chellerosemercy*
2. *Finding Mercy www.books2read.com/chellerosefinding-mercy*
3. *Liam and Mercy www.books2read.com/LiamandMercy*
4. *Xander's Secret https://books2read.com/Xanderssecret*

Dark Desires Series

1. *Unholy www.books2read.com/chelleroseunholy*
2. *Unhinged www.books2read.com/chelleroseunhinged*
3. *Unchained www.books2read.com/chelleroseunchained*
4. *Undone www.books2read.com/chelleroseundone*
5. *An Unhinged Wedding*
   www.books2read.com/unhingedwedding

Men of Mayhem Series

1. *De Luca: The Devil* www.books2read.com/delucathedevil
2. *De Luca: The Saint* www.books2read.com/delucasaint
3. *De Luca: The Sinister Game*
   www.books2read.com/sinistergame
4. De Luca: The Dalia Effect
   www.books2read.com/thedaliaeffect

Den of Sin Duet

1. Zade www.books2read.com/zade
2. Sin www.books2read.com/sin-chellerose

Bonetti Brothers Series

1. Bones www.books2read.com/boneschellerose
2. Reaper www.books2read.com/reaper-chellerose

Printed in Dunstable, United Kingdom

67172247R00143